Dear Reader,

Holidays, for women, are not necessarily the best time to get any visiting done. I know that my mother, sisters and I usually spend all our time in the kitchen, either cooking for or cleaning up after the herd of relatives who gather for the holidays, making it impossible for us to spend any "quality" time together. To resolve this, we began reserving one weekend a year for a mother-daughter getaway. Now we've expanded our getaways to include our own daughters, making these a three-generation event.

No matter what location we choose for our getaways, we always try to stay at a bed-and-breakfast. We enjoy the warmth and coziness a B & B offers us, plus the food is always to die for. One of our favorites is the Lucky Penny Ranch B & B, near Austin, Texas. The views from the deck are breathtaking and the peacefulness of the country setting allows us lots of time to kick back and just talk.

Because of my love for bed-and-breakfasts, I thought it would be fun to write a book about one, knowing the possibilities for romance would be endless...and titillating! I hope you enjoy *A Willful Marriage*. The characters and the setting may be fictional, but the ambience the setting offers is real and can be found at B & B's throughout the world!

Peggy Moreland

Heading to the Hitchin' Post

1. *Unforgettable Bride* by Annette Broadrick
2. *Precious Pretender* by Stella Bagwell
3. *Mail-Order Brood* by Arlene James
4. *A Willful Marriage* by Peggy Moreland
5. *Her Kind of Man* by Barbara McCauley
6. *Storming Paradise* by Mary McBride

He's a Cowboy!

7. *Christmas Kisses for a Dollar* by Laurie Paige
8. *Lone Wolf's Lady* by Beverly Barton
9. *Love, Honor and a Pregnant Bride* by Karen Rose Smith
10. *Some Kind of Hero* by Sandy Steen
11. *The Cowboy Takes a Lady* by Cindy Gerard
12. *The Outlaw and the City Slicker* by Debbi Rawlins

Lone Star Lullabies

13. *Texas Baby* by Joan Elliott Pickart
14. *Like Father, Like Son* by Elizabeth August
15. *Mike's Baby* by Mary Lynn Baxter
16. *Long Lost Husband* by Joleen Daniels
17. *Cowboy Cootchie-Coo* by Tina Leonard
18. *Daddy Was a Cowboy* by Jodi O'Donnell

Texas Tycoons

19. *The Water Baby* by Roz Denny Fox
20. *Too Many Bosses* by Jan Freed
21. *Two Brothers and a Bride* by Elizabeth Harbison
22. *Call Me* by Alison Kent
23. *One Ticket to Texas* by Jan Hudson
24. *His-and-Hers Family* by Bonnie K. Winn

Feisty Fillies

25. *A Girl's Best Friend* by Marie Ferrarella
26. *Bedded Bliss* by Heather MacAllister
27. *The Guardian's Bride* by Laurie Paige
28. *Millie and the Fugitive* by Liz Ireland
29. *My Baby, Your Child* by Nikki Benjamin
30. *Hannah's Hunks* by Bonnie Tucker

Trouble in Texas

31. *Guilty as Sin* by Cathy Gillen Thacker
32. *Family Ties* by Joanna Wayne
33. *Familiar Heart* by Caroline Burnes
34. *Double Vision* by Sheryl Lynn
35. *The Loner and the Lady* by Eileen Wilks
36. *Wild Innocence* by Ann Major

Men Most Wanted

37. *Lawman* by Laurie Grant
38. *Texas Lawman* by Ginger Chambers
39. *It Happened in Texas* by Darlene Graham
40. *Satan's Angel* by Kristin James
41. *The Lone Ranger* by Sharon De Vita
42. *Hide in Plain Sight* by Sara Orwig

Cuddlin' Kin

43. *West Texas Weddings* by Ginger Chambers
44. *A Mother for Jeffrey* by Trisha Alexander
45. *Desperate* by Kay David
46. *Father in the Middle* by Phyllis Halldorson
47. *The Texas Touch* by Kate Thomas
48. *Child of Her Heart* by Arlene James

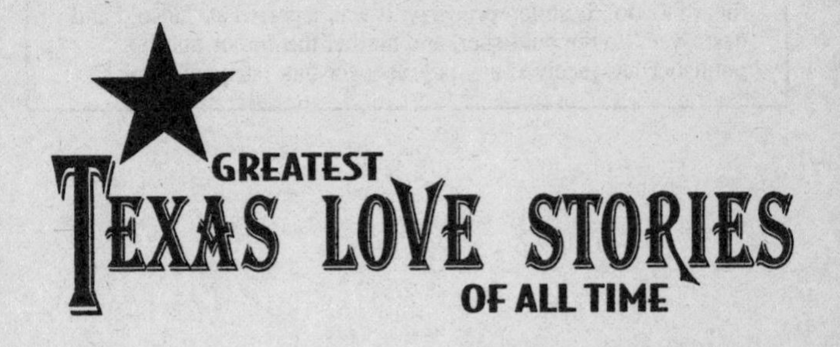

A WILLFUL MARRIAGE

Peggy Moreland

Heading to the Hitchin' Post

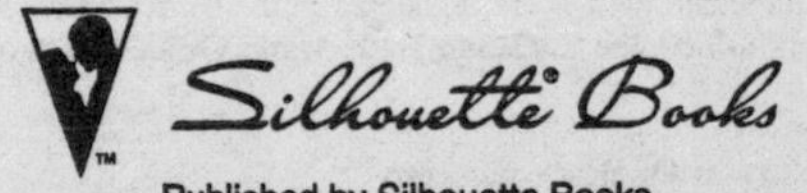

Published by Silhouette Books
America's Publisher of Contemporary Romance

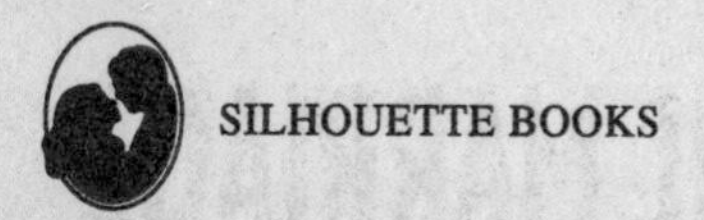

ISBN 0-373-65218-6

A WILLFUL MARRIAGE

This edition published by arrangement with Harlequin Books S.A.

Visit Silhouette at www.eHarlequin.com

Printed in U.S.A.

PEGGY MORELAND

published her first romance with Silhouette in 1989 and continues to delight readers with stories set in her home state of Texas. Winner of the National Reviewers' Choice Award, a nominee for *Romantic Times* Reviewers' Choice Award, and a two-time finalist for the prestigious RITA® Award, Peggy's books frequently appear on the *USA TODAY* and Waldenbooks' bestseller lists. When not writing, you can usually find Peggy outside, tending the cattle, goats and other critters on the ranch she shares with her husband. You may write to Peggy at P.O. Box 1099, Florence, TX 76527-1099, or e-mail her at peggy@peggymoreland.com.

Books by Peggy Moreland

Silhouette Desire

A Little Bit Country #515
Run for the Roses #598
Miss Prim #682
The Rescuer #765
Seven Year Itch #837
The Baby Doctor #867
Miss Lizzy's Legacy #921
A Willful Marriage #1024
**Marry Me, Cowboy* #1084
**A Little Texas Two-Step* #1090
**Lone Star Kind of Man* #1096
†*The Rancher's Spittin' Image* #1156
†*The Restless Virgin* #1163
†*A Sparkle in the Cowboy's Eyes* #1168
†*That McCloud Woman* #1227
Billionaire Bridegroom #1244
†*Hard Lovin' Man* #1270
‡*Ride a Wild Heart* #1306
‡*In Name Only* #1313
‡*Slow Waltz Across Texas* #1315
Groom of Fortune #1336
The Way to a Rancher's Heart #1345
Millionaire Boss #1365
The Texan's Tiny Secret #1394
Her Lone Star Protector #1426

Silhouette Special Edition

Rugrats and Rawhide #1084

Silhouette Books

Turning Point 2002
"It Had To Be You"

*Trouble in Texas
†Texas Brides
‡Texas Grooms

In everyone's life there is that special teacher
they never forget. For me, there are several.
To Cheryl Rahmlow, who ruled the hallowed halls of
Terrell High School with both discipline and love
and who taught me how to type. To Della Jo Burnes,
who followed me from elementary school to high school
and on to junior college, just to make sure I got it right.
And to Eldora Birdsong, who made Shakespeare come
alive with her "special effects." Thanks, ladies,
for all the years you devoted to teaching and the
difference you made in so many of your students' lives.

One

It was a miserable day for a funeral.

Gray skies heavy with the threat of rain loomed overhead while a bitterly cold wind blew from the north, rattling the stripped tree branches like the bones of a dancing skeleton.

Considering the man being buried, though, Brett Sinclair figured the weather was more than appropriate. Coldhearted, stingy, unforgiving. Yes, the more he thought about it, the more he was sure that the old man deserved just such a day.

He sat behind the wheel of his truck at the end of the line of cars forming the funeral procession, working up a strong defense in favor of staying inside the vehicle instead of joining the mourners graveside. No one knew him, he told himself, so his presence certainly wouldn't be missed.

While he sat debating, the wind caught a corner of the funeral home's canvas canopy, inflating its gently sloping roof and dumping sheets of icy rain onto the mourners who stood under its edge. A shiver chased down his spine. That was an even better reason to remain inside—it was colder than a well-digger's butt out there. Besides, he told himself, he'd had his share of funerals. First his father's, then his mother's, and now this.

With a muffled growl, he shouldered open the door. He hadn't traveled this far to sit in the warmth of his truck. He'd come to witness the old man's burial. The wind caught his duster and billowed it open, sending icy needles of cold to stab at his chest. He quickly did up two buttons, scrunched his shoulders to his ears and headed for the tight cluster of black umbrellas near the fringe of the funeral home's canopy. He stopped at the rear of the cemetery plot, close enough to hear, but far enough away to avoid being a part of the ceremony. He listened dispassionately as the minister spoke kindly of the man being laid to rest. The fact that every word coming out of the preacher's mouth was a bald-faced lie didn't really bother Brett. After all, how much truth was found in any eulogy?

He soon grew bored with the proceedings and let his gaze wander beneath the canopy. Sprays of gladiolus and carnations propped on easels formed a semicircle around the raised casket, their spring colors a strong contrast to the bleak landscape surrounding it.

The casket itself bore a blanket of yellow roses. Inside, he knew, lay his grandfather. Brett waited a moment, testing himself to see if he felt anything. A glimmer of recognition. A stab of grief. A sliver of regret. But nothing came. Not one blessed thing.

With a philosophical shrug, he let his gaze move on. A couple of rows of folding chairs beneath the canopy seated those who had arrived early enough not to have to stand out in the cold. None of the chairs' occupants appeared to be less than seventy years of age.

Except one.

His gaze settled on the woman in the front row—the area usually reserved for family. Although people stood on the perimeter of the tent huddled under dripping umbrellas and shaking from the cold, the seats on either side of her remained empty. She was a striking woman; young, dressed all in black. Her hair was the color of spun gold, a halo of sunshine riding a sea of black.

Even from his distance, he could see that her eyes were red and puffy from crying, but she kept her shoulders straight, her chin high and her eyes on the minister who was now reading from the Bible. Occasionally, her gaze would slip to the casket and her eyes would fill. Quickly she would look away, back to the minister, in an obvious attempt to keep the grief at bay.

Something about the woman pulled at Brett, and he found he couldn't look away. Although others might be swayed by the fact that she was crying, he knew that wasn't what held him. He'd had years to become immune to the debilitating power of a woman's tears.

What was it about her that was so intriguing? he wondered. Maybe it was the way she held herself, he decided, her chin lifted just a fraction higher than good posture required. As he studied her, he couldn't help wondering whether it was pride or defiance that kept her chin at that angle.

Being isolated as she was from the other mourners only added to the mystique that surrounded her. Brett knew if he were sitting in a bar or roaming a cocktail party instead of standing on the edge of a cemetery plot, he would already have made his move.

Who was she? he wondered. As far as he knew, Ned Parker had no relatives to grieve over his passing—other than himself, of course, but Brett didn't consider himself a relative. It took more than blood to make a family, and blood was all they had between them. By his estimation, the old man would have been about eighty-three, and this woman couldn't be much more than twenty-five, so it would be ridiculous to think she'd been a friend.... Or maybe she had been a friend of sorts, he thought, as a new possibility surfaced. Like a mistress, maybe. From what his mother had told him, it would be like the old goat to keep a young woman around to entertain him.

And now, here the woman sat in front of the whole town, grieving for a man old enough to be her grandfather. His suspicions rose a notch higher. Maybe she was crying because with his death, her life of leisure and luxury was at an end. He knew the old man was worth a bundle. His mother had told him that. But she'd also told him how stingy he was. He wondered if that stinginess extended to his mistresses. If so, then maybe she was putting on a show to win the town's sympathy in hopes that if the true heirs didn't show up, she could get her hands on his money.

He turned away in disgust. As far as he was concerned, she could have it all.

At the last amen, signaling the end of the service, Gayla lifted her head and stood on rubbery legs numbed by the cold. She took the hand the minister offered and squeezed her gratitude. "Thank you, Reverend Brown. I know Ned would have been pleased with your remarks."

The reverend patted their joined hands. "I doubt it," he whispered for her ears only. "But one can always hope." The comment was so full of the truth, Gayla couldn't help but smile, for Ned Parker probably wouldn't have been pleased to hear kind words spoken over his grave. If he'd had his way, he would have been buried in a pine box with no one but the gravediggers on hand for the ceremony. But Gayla had been equally determined that he would receive a proper and Christian burial, and the Reverend Mark Brown had honored her request.

With a last squeeze of her hand, the reverend stepped aside to let the rest of the mourners pass by the casket for one final view. A few offered their hands to Gayla, but most ignored her presence. Their coolness didn't offend her; she'd had years to grow accustomed to the town's constant censure.

The sight of the last man in line, though, drew a quivering smile. John Thomas, Ned's attorney. John had served as Ned's attorney for more than twelve years, ever since the death of John's own father who had originally carried the responsibility.

When John reached her, he not only took her hand, but drew her against his chest for a tight hug. The tears that Gayla had fought throughout the service broke through.

She stepped away, dabbing at her eyes and cheeks. She dragged in a shuddery breath, keeping her arm at John's waist while angling her body so that they both faced the casket. "I can't believe he's gone."

"Neither can I." Gayla tightened her hold on him, sharing his sorrow and offering silent support. "The old codger put up a good fight, didn't he?" he said gruffly.

Fresh tears welled and Gayla could only nod her agreement.

John's chest rose and fell in a deep sigh. "Heaven will never be the same," he said with a shake of his head. "He's probably already got a poker game going and is stripping the angels of their golden harps while he calmly smokes one of those damn stinking cigars of his."

Gayla couldn't help but laugh, for John was probably right. She looked up at him, grateful to him for giving her a reason to smile when her world seemed to be crashing down around her. "Thanks, John. You've been a good friend, to Ned and to me."

"And I'm still here for you. Don't forget that," he warned, shaking a finger beneath her nose.

"I won't."

The gravediggers appeared, anxious to finish their work and get out of the cold. Unable to watch this final scene, Gayla turned away. John seemed to understand her need to escape. He took her elbow and they walked in silence to the waiting car. "Have you heard from Ned's daughter?" she asked, trying her best to keep her tone light and free of the fears that nagged at her.

John frowned. "No, though I'd hoped she'd at least have the decency to come to the funeral."

"Ned always said she wouldn't come, even for that. I guess he was right." At the car door, she paused, not wanting to ask, but needing an answer to the question that still plagued her. "When will I need to move?"

John opened the door for her, a frown furrowing his forehead. "Don't you worry about that now. Until Ned's daughter shows up to claim her inheritance, there's no need to make any changes. When you feel up to it, open Parker House for guests again. We'll take care of the rest as the need arises. But for now," he said, urging her into the car, "why don't you go home and get out of the cold? You'll feel better once you've had some rest."

Brett had gone to the cemetery on a whim. Why, he wasn't sure. The old man meant nothing to him.

Yet, for some reason the service had left him restless and out of sorts. Eventually hunger drew him to a restaurant where he stopped to grab a bite to eat before finding a place to stay the night.

On the way inside, he plucked a local newspaper from a rack for company during his meal. Once the waitress had seated him and he'd placed his order, he settled back to thumb through the pages. Most of the front-page news was local stuff. On the second page, though, a headline caught his eye. Services Scheduled For Longtime Braesburg Resident. The obituary carried a picture, although anyone's photograph could have been placed there and Brett wouldn't have known the difference. He'd never seen his grandfather in person and if his mother had owned a picture of the man, she'd never shown it to Brett.

He read the article more out of boredom than anything else. Member of the Chamber of Commerce, Kiwanis Club. It appears the old man was at least civically, if not family oriented, he thought with no little malice. Preceded in death by his wife, Marjorie Holmes Parker. No mention of any survivors, but then Brett hadn't expected the old man to mention his daughter. Why would he claim her after his death when he'd refused to acknowledge her while he was alive?

No. 1 Oak Knoll. The address listed as his residence sounded snobbish. Probably was. The one thing his mother had told him about Ned Parker was how proud he was of that property.

And now Brett owned it and everything else the old man had left behind.

As he stared at the paper, seeing nothing but the headaches associated with the unwanted inheritance, the solution to all his problems slowly came to him. Wouldn't it be the perfect irony if he gave it all away to some charity? The property that the man had valued more than his daughter's love? That would surely make the old man turn over in his grave! The thought brought the first smile that had creased his face since receiving the news of his grandfather's death.

His dinner arrived and along with it, his appetite. He mentally laid out a plan of action while he ate. He would go to the attorney's office first thing the next morning and get all the legal technicalities taken care of. He would simply give it all to—

He dropped his fork to his plate in disgust, as the need to make yet another decision arose. Which charity should he leave it to? he wondered in growing consternation. There were plenty out there to choose from. He glanced at the newspaper beside his plate and noticed that the city council was meeting that night.

The city, he thought with a satisfied smile. He would give it all to the city. They would probably turn it into a day-care center or a parking lot or maybe even tear it down. That would really get the old man's goat. The house and whatever property the old man had left meant nothing to Brett. He just wanted to be done with this unwanted responsibility and head back home.

He left the restaurant satisfied with his plan and sure

that once he checked into a motel, he would sleep like a baby—something he hadn't been able to do since he'd received the news of his grandfather's death.

He was driving down Main Street looking for a place to spend the night, when he saw the street sign indicating Oak Knoll. Curious, he made the turn.

He assumed the street had received its name from the oaks that lined it. They arched across the wide avenue to form a natural canopy overhead. The houses sat way back on lots of an acre or more, and through the bare tree branches he could see that lights shone from a few of the residences. He glanced at the clock on the dash and was surprised to see that it was almost six o'clock. He hadn't slept in almost forty-eight hours. He would see the house, he told himself, then he was going to find a place to spend the night.

He followed the street to where it ended in a wide cul-de-sac. At the curb a stone pillar held a mailbox and below it swung a sign. No. 1 Oak Knoll, Parker House Bed-and-Breakfast.

He puckered his forehead in confusion. A bed-and-breakfast? Surely, he'd made a mistake. The newspaper lay on the seat beside him and he flipped it open to verify the address mentioned in the obituary.

A bed-and-breakfast? He couldn't believe the old man would share his house with strangers when he wasn't even willing to share it with his daughter.

He didn't think twice about turning into the drive. It was a business, after all, so who could complain? Floodlights situated around the perimeter of the house made seeing the two-story native stone structure easy through the light fog and drizzling rain.

All of the mental pictures that he'd had of his mother's former home slowly went up in smoke. He'd expected something dark and menacing, straight out of a gothic novel—nothing at all like this. Even through the rain and gloom that hung over it, the house still managed to look homey, even cheerful.

Wicker furniture was scattered about the wide front porch and the balcony above it. Dark green shutters flanked the windows that stretched from the floor of the porch to its ceiling. Through them, he could just make out the glow of a light coming from the rear of the house.

He'd meant to drive up to the house, take a quick look, then head out. If asked later, he couldn't have said what made him climb out of his truck and approach the house. He rang the doorbell and waited, hunching his shoulders against the cold, wondering if anyone would respond to the bell and what he would say if they did.

Light from fixtures on either side of the door popped on and the door swung open. A woman stepped into the wedge of light. Although her face was washed free of makeup and her hair pulled up in a disheveled knot, he immediately recognized her as the young woman he'd seen at the cemetery.

The sight of her drew the same knee-jerk response he'd experienced earlier when he'd seen her at the funeral. Rather than the all-black garb she'd worn then, she now wore a shapeless denim dress that hung nearly to her ankles. The toes of her bare feet curled against the cold.

"May I help you?" she asked politely.

"Yes," he replied. "I'd like a room for the night."

She seemed startled by the request, then gestured to a white bow adorning the door. "I'm sorry, but we aren't open for business," she said in apology. "Mr. Parker passed away and was buried just this afternoon."

Brett tried his darnedest to look remorseful. "I'm sorry. I had no idea. And I was looking forward to staying here." He hunched his shoulders closer to his ears as a gust of wind swept across the wide porch. "I don't know my way around town, so if you would be kind enough to direct me to a hotel or motel where I might get a room for the night, I'd be obliged."

She hesitated only slightly, then opened the door wider, inviting him in. "It's a nasty night to be out," she said and closed the door behind him.

"Yes, ma'am, it is," he agreed as he took this unexpected opportunity to look around. The entry was wide and welcoming, with a long upholstered bench along one side and a library table on the other. In front of him a staircase stretched upward into the darkness. He looked for some sign that his mother had once lived there—a photograph, anything—but saw nothing.

"We keep a phone here for the convenience of our guests," she told him as she crossed to a table and pulled open a drawer. She took out a thick directory, flipped to the Yellow Pages, then gestured for him to join her. "Other than Parker House, Braesburg only has a motel, and unfortunately, it's closed for repair. The closest place will be in Austin and that's a good hour's drive." She frowned and tapped the page of the Austin directory. "But you might have a difficult time driving there tonight. I heard on the news a few minutes ago that they're predicting an ice storm. Unusual for this part of Texas, but coming our way nonetheless."

He tried to appear properly crestfallen. "Do you have any other suggestions?"

"Not really," she said, worrying her lower lip as she stole a glance his way. She must have noticed the weariness of his stance or the dark circles under his eyes, for she closed the book with a decided snap. "I can't very well send you out on a night like this. You can stay here."

"I wouldn't want to impose."

"Your staying here wouldn't be an imposition." She pushed back a wisp of hair that had escaped her bun, exposing a wan smile shaped by full, moist lips. "In fact, I'd welcome the company."

"You're sure?" he asked hesitantly.

"Positive." With the decision made, she replaced the directory and shut the drawer. She angled the guest book his way. "If you'll sign in here, Mr.—" She looked up at him inquiringly.

"Sinclair," he said without thinking. "Brett Sinclair," he finished more slowly. He extended his hand, watching her face for some sign of recognition.

But her facial expression never changed. She simply

accepted his hand, smiled softly and replied, "Gayla Matthews. It's nice to meet you."

After he'd entered his name, she closed the register. "If you'd like, you can park under the portico in the back and get your things while I prepare a room for you."

"No need to go to any trouble."

"No trouble. Use the kitchen door just off the portico. There's a pot of coffee on the stove in the kitchen. Help yourself."

Without further ado, she caught up the fabric of her dress and climbed the stairs. Brett stood at the foot of the staircase and watched, her every step awarding him a more revealing view of her bare legs. Long, graceful, well shaped, he could almost imagine the feel of them wrapped around him. He shook his head, dispelling the image. What in the world had come over him? This woman was his grandfather's mistress, for God's sake!

He continued to watch until she reached the landing and disappeared down the dark hall, and wondered at his own sanity.

A night in his grandfather's house with his grandfather's mistress. What in the hell had possessed him to ask for a room? He shook his head at his own stupidity and headed out the front door.

Brett poured himself a cup of coffee, nursing its warmth between his hands as he rested a hip against the countertop and stared over his shoulder out the kitchen window. Outside sleet fell, exposed in the glow of the security light above the garage. The weatherman had been right, he acknowledged ruefully. The ice storm had arrived and in a matter of hours, the roads would be closed. Thanks to Gayla's generosity, though, he wouldn't be caught out in it.

Gayla? Generous? He sipped his coffee, puzzling over that particular possibility. At least in this instance she was, he amended. She might not be so accommodating when she learned who he was and his plans for Parker House.

He shook his head as he thought about her. It was hard for him to believe that she was his grandfather's mistress, but he couldn't think of any other plausible explanation for her presence at Parker House or the extent of her grief. Although he didn't have much to commend his grandfather for, he could certainly salute his taste in women. Gayla was slender—he had detected that much through the shapeless dress—yet blessed with enough curves to satisfy any man's tastes.

"I see you found the coffeepot."

Brett jumped at the sound of her voice, fearful that somehow she'd managed to read his thoughts. He forced himself to take a deep breath before he turned to fully face her. He shifted the small of his back to rest against the countertop and lifted the cup in salute. "I did. And thanks." He tipped his head in the direction of the window behind him. "It seems the weatherman was right, for a change. It's already sleeting." He offered her a grateful smile. "If not for you, I'd probably be stuck on the side of some road out there, freezing."

She waved away his thanks. ''Never turn away a guest,'' she said as if quoting some unwritten law. At his puzzled look, she explained, ''An innkeeper's rule for survival.'' She crossed to the coffeepot and poured a cup for herself. ''Have you eaten? I could prepare something for you, if you like.''

''Thanks, but I grabbed a bite at a café on Main Street before I came here.''

''Dessert, then?'' she asked. ''I made a pound cake this morning, just in case—'' She stopped herself before confessing she'd baked the cake in hopes that Ned's daughter would show up for the funeral. When Brett continued to look at her, waiting for her to finish the statement, she blushed and turned away.

''In case what?'' he pressed.

''In case any of the mourners came by after the funeral,'' she finished lamely. She set her cup aside and busied herself gathering plates and silverware.

Brett couldn't resist asking, ''Did anyone come?''

''No,'' she replied, her voice carrying a tinge of disappointment. ''I'm sure it was the weather that kept them away.'' She turned to him and forced a cheerful smile. ''But you're here, so it won't go to waste. If you'll have a piece, that is?''

And how could he refuse when she looked at him that way, obviously not wanting to be alone? He nodded his agreement. ''Can't let a good pound cake go to waste, now, can we?''

He pushed away from the sink and followed her to the table. She lifted off the domed top of a crystal cake plate, cut a generous slice of cake and levered it onto a dessert plate. Her movements were graceful and sure as she moved to the refrigerator and removed two bowls. From one she poured a measure of thick strawberry sauce onto the cake and from the other, a dollop of whipped cream. In spite of the fact that he wasn't one bit hungry, Brett's mouth watered as she slipped the plate in front of him. She stepped back, folding her hands neatly at her waist. "Would you care for anything else?"

Brett picked up his fork and gestured to the chair opposite his. "Sit down and join me. I hate to eat alone."

She sat—although he could tell she would rather have fussed around the kitchen—and twisted a napkin she plucked from the table between her fingers. He toyed with his fork and tried like hell to think of something to say to fill the awkward silence. He finally took a bite of the cake. "This is real tasty. Do you do the cooking around here?"

"Thank you and, yes, I'm the cook." She laughed softly. "And the upstairs maid and the downstairs maid and the concierge and the gardener."

He lifted his gaze, his jaw slack with surprise. "You mean you do it all? There's no staff?"

"No one other than myself, but really there's no need. Business is usually slow in the winter months. In the summer, if we are booked for several weeks, I'll hire a temporary to help out with the cleaning, but for the most part, I can handle the work.

"That's what makes a bed-and-breakfast so appealing," she explained. "People want to feel as if they are staying in a home, not a hotel. And that's what I try to provide. Home-cooked meals, served in a warm and homey environment."

Her sincerity and enthusiasm for Parker House and her job surprised him. It also drew a few questions. Like, how did she find the time—or the energy, for that matter—to serve as the old man's mistress if she had all the responsibilities of running the place? From what he could see, the place was huge.

"How many guests can you put up at a time?"

"There are six guest rooms, plus, last year we remodeled the carriage house and turned it into a bridal suite for honeymooners. It's more private and there is a little sitting area off the back with a hot tub. It makes a romantic setting on a summer night."

He absorbed all this, wondering how he could establish her relationship with Ned without asking outright. "Has the house been in your family long?"

She looked surprised, then quickly shook her head. "The house doesn't belong to me. I just work here. The house is—" She swallowed and amended, "*Was* Mr. Parker's."

"The man who was buried today?"

"Yes." She rose, picking up her still-full coffee cup, and carried it to the sink.

"What will happen now that he's gone?"

Her back to him, she lifted a shoulder. "That's up to his heirs."

"Do they live in Braesburg?" Brett asked, wanting to see how much Gayla knew about his family.

"No," she replied as she ran water into the cup.

"I'm not sure where they live. Mr. Parker never spoke much about them. His attorney is handling all that."

She finished washing out the cup and laid it gently on the drainboard. She stared out the window for a moment, her wrists resting on the sink's edge, her shoulders slumped as if weighted by an unusually heavy burden. Then she seemed to shake herself from whatever thoughts she'd been focused on, and plucked a dish towel from the drainboard. She slowly dried her hands as she turned. "Would you like to see the rest of the house?" she asked, all signs of the melancholy gone. "I can give you a quick tour, then show you your room."

Brett shoved back from the table, anxious to see more of the house his mother had grown up in. "Yes, ma'am, I would." He retrieved his duffel bag from where he'd left it by the back door, then followed her through the kitchen door and out into the hall.

"The house was built in the 1830s," she told him, as they walked to the front entry, "by Mrs. Parker's family. They were of German descent, as were most of the town's residents." She stopped at the arched doorway that led into the living room and flipped on a light switch. A grand piano dominated one corner, while the rest of the space was sectioned into several cozy sitting areas, each with an antique sofa and a couple of overstuffed chairs.

"The furnishings, for the most part, are all original pieces, some brought to this country from Germany by Mrs. Parker's family. Our guests are free to gather in here...play the piano, read, or just relax." She switched off the light and crossed the hall to a large dining room, with Brett following close at her heels.

She flipped another switch and twin chandeliers flickered on above a long mahogany table.

"Most of our more formal meals are served in the dining room, although when the weather is nice, I like to serve breakfasts in the garden room." She switched off the light and motioned for Brett to follow her. "The garden room is my personal favorite. It's smaller and more intimate. When we decided to convert Parker House into a bed-and-breakfast," she explained as she pushed back pocket doors, "I had the back porch enclosed." She switched on the light.

Brett felt as if he'd stepped into a summer garden. Floor-to-ceiling windows dominated three walls. The fourth was painted a pale yellow. Trails of hand-painted ivy framed the windows and crept onto the ceiling, giving the room its garden theme. Three round tables filled the center of the room, each draped with brightly colored floral cloths. The same fabric was swagged above each window, giving the effect of flowers coming into full bloom. An antique buffet stretched the length of the only solid wall, holding place mats, a coffee maker and a wooden basket filled with silverware and napkins.

Brett looked at Gayla and noticed the pride that showed in her eyes. "You did this, didn't you?"

"The remodeling?" She shook her head. "No, I'm no carpenter by any stretch of the imagination. I just did the painting and sewed the drapes and the tablecloths. We hired a local man to enclose the room."

She made her contribution sound so slight, but Brett could see that it was her touch that gave the room its ambience.

"Would you like to see the upstairs now?" she asked politely.

Brett shifted his duffel bag to his other hand. "Yes, ma'am, if you don't mind."

He followed Gayla back into the hall and then up the stairs.

On the landing, Gayla stopped in front of the door at the top of the stairs. "This will be your room, but I'll save it for last." She turned down the hall to her left. "There are three rooms in this wing of the house and four in the other, with your room separating them."

She stopped in front of the first, chuckling, and tapped a finger on the brass plate attached to the front of the door. "It was Ned's idea to name each room after Texas politicians. He insisted on putting all the Democrats on the left and the Republicans on the right, to keep them from fighting, he said."

So he had a sense of humor, Brett thought, unmoved by this new knowledge. He followed Gayla into the right wing, only half listening as she expounded on Parker House's history. At the end of the hall she stopped, her hand resting on the knob of the last door. Unlike the other rooms, no brass plate marked this door. Brett looked at her inquiringly.

Gayla dropped her hand to her side, her eyes bright with tears. "This was Mr. Parker's room," she said in explanation, then turned away.

She quickly moved to the door at the head of the stairs that she had told Brett would be his for the night, appearing anxious now to end the tour. ''This room was named for Ned's wife, Marjorie. Ned always referred to her as 'the peacemaker,' thus her placement here between the two parties. From what I've learned about her from Ned and others, she was a gentle woman, soft-spoken, but with a knack for handling even the most stubborn individuals. Being married to Ned, I'm sure that came in handy. He was devoted to her.''

A devoted husband? Brett thought, stifling a snort of disgust. Not according to the stories he'd been told by his mother.

Gayla opened the door and quickly crossed to switch on the lamp beside the bed. ''I think you'll be comfortable in this room. You have a private bath, there,'' she told him, pointing to a door at her right. ''Linens are in the closet behind the door.''

She turned to him, looking suddenly tired and anxious to escape his presence. ''If you'll excuse me,'' she said as she twisted her hands at her waist. ''I think I'll go on to bed now. Help yourself to more coffee in the kitchen. There's a television in the study. Stay up as late as you'd like. We like our guests to feel at home.''

Brett watched her until she closed the door behind her, blocking his view. *At home?* he thought with a snort. Not in this lifetime, and certainly not in this house.

Two

Although he hadn't slept in over two days, Brett lay on his back on the feather bed in the room Gayla had prepared for him, wide-awake, his fingers laced beneath his head. He stared at the ceiling, hoping and praying that sleep would come soon. His entire body ached with weariness.

When he'd received the message to call his mother's attorney, he'd just returned from an exhausting three-state inspection of all the Sinclair department stores. He'd been tempted to ignore the call, at least until he'd gotten some rest, but then had decided not to put it off. Now he wished he had waited.

The attorney was the one who had given him the news of his grandfather's death. He'd said he'd received a telegram from an attorney in Braesburg,

Texas, notifying him of the old man's death and requesting that Christine, Brett's mother, come home for the funeral.

Brett had almost laughed at that. So the old man had wanted his daughter to come home. His request had come too late. Christine Sinclair wouldn't be coming home. Not ever again. Brett had buried her less than six months before.

The attorney had then reminded him that as Christine's heir, he would inherit his grandfather's estate.

That was worth a laugh, as well. Brett didn't want the old man's money. Why should he? The old man had never bothered to acknowledge his family before.

He would have ended the conversation then and gone to bed, but the attorney had insisted that he attend the funeral, saying that he owed it to his mother to do so. Brett disagreed with that bit of logic, but had finally gotten the attorney off his back by telling him he would give the lawyer in Braesburg a call after he'd had some rest.

But for some reason he'd found he couldn't sleep. In the end, he'd thrown some clothes into a duffel bag and climbed back into his truck and headed for Braesburg. He'd driven all night and part of the next day, arriving just as the funeral procession was heading for the cemetery.

And now here he was in his grandfather's house, wide-awake and with his ulcer burning a hole in his stomach. On a weary sigh, he dragged another pillow beneath his head, then leaned to turn on the bedside lamp. He fell back against the pillow and looked around the room. Nice little touches were scattered about, obviously Gayla's work—a basket of fruit and crackers on the bedside table, a porcelain dish filled with green and pink mints. A pitcher of ice water. A crystal glass. He leaned over and thumbed up the lid on the pitcher, then promptly fell back against the pillows, unconsciously rubbing his hand across his stomach. No, water wasn't what he needed. He needed milk to ease the burning.

She'd said for him to make himself at home, he remembered. He levered himself from the bed and hoped she'd included raiding the refrigerator in that invitation. He pulled on his jeans, but didn't bother with his shirt and boots, then headed downstairs.

Careful not to make any noise, he eased down the stairs and across the hall. He was almost to the kitchen door when he heard a noise. He hesitated, listening, and was sure the sound had come from behind the study door. Thinking maybe he'd forgotten to turn off the television, he quickly crossed to the study and pushed open the door but froze when he saw Gayla sitting in an old leather chair by the fireplace, her back to him, bent at the waist, rocking back and forth. White-knuckled fingers clutched the ties of her robe against her mouth, muffling her sobs. He took a cautious step back, meaning to leave her to her grief, but then he stopped, his heart squeezing in time with each rise and fall of her slender shoulders.

She shouldn't be alone at a time like this, he told himself angrily. She ought to have family or friends here to share her grief.

He took a step closer.

"Ma'am? Is something wrong?"

She whirled at the sound of his voice, then lurched to her feet. "No," she said, swiping at her tears. "Nothing's wrong. I couldn't sleep and I—" She pressed the back of her hand against her mouth to stifle the sob that rose.

She looked about ready to collapse. Brett pressed her back into the chair. "You just sit down there and rest a minute. Can I get you something? A glass of warm milk? A shot of whiskey?"

"No—no, really," she stammered, pulling the folds of her robe across her knees. "I'm sorry I awakened you."

"You didn't wake me. I couldn't sleep, either." Wearily, he dropped down on the floor beside the chair and pulled his knees against his chest, trying to think what to do. "Is there someone in your family that I can call? You know, to keep you company?"

She squeezed her hands between her knees, unable to meet his gaze. She shook her head. "No. No one."

A shiver shook Brett clear to his toes at the bleakness in her tone. "It's cold in here," he said, blaming his reaction, in case she'd noticed, on the chill in the room.

"I'm sorry," she said, instantly apologetic. "I turn the heat down on the first floor after I go to bed. But if you're cold," she said, rising to her feet, "I can turn it up."

Brett caught her hand and pulled her back into the chair. He'd never seen a woman so intent to please.

"How about if I just light that stack of wood in the fireplace? That ought to take the chill off."

"I can do it."

Brett laid a hand on her arm before she could rise. "And so can I," he said firmly.

Seeing the stubborn glint in his eye, Gayla reluctantly sat. She watched as he carefully prepared the fire. The flame caught, then rose higher. Picking up the poker, Brett punched at the wood, rearranging it on the grate.

The fire's glow radiated off his bare chest, capturing the gold in a necklace that swung from his neck. From the necklace's delicate links hung a thin gold band and with each jab of his arm, the necklace swung, the band slapping against first one muscled pec, then the other.

Gayla had never really considered herself sexually deprived, but at the moment she couldn't take her eyes off the sight of so much raw maleness. His shoulders were broad and muscled, tapering down to a slim waist and hips. *A cowboy's butt,* she decided a little breathlessly, noticing the way his jeans cupped his rear end. She'd heard the bawdy phrase at Betty Jo's Beauty Salon, but had never seen anything that fit the description quite so appropriately.

His skin glowed in the firelight, taking on a coppery hue, and she had the most irresistible urge to lay her hand on his back and feel the play of muscle as he poked and shoved at the dry wood. But thankfully, before she could act on the impulse, he replaced the poker and scooted back to sit beside her chair.

After a few moments, Brett tipped his head up to

look at her. "What were you doing down here, anyway?"

His question brought the grief rushing back. "I don't know," she replied, swallowing the threat of more tears. "Lonely, I guess." She dipped her head, embarrassed by the admission. "Ned spent most of his time in this room. Being here just seemed to make him closer."

Brett turned his gaze back to the fire. "I used to do the same thing," he replied thoughtfully.

Surprised, she tipped her head to look at him. "Really?"

"Yeah, after my mother passed away, I'd slip into her bedroom, just to get the scent of her. Eased the loneliness a bit."

She nodded knowingly, a wistful smile playing at the corners of her mouth. "No perfume smells here, though. Ned smoked the most god-awful-smelling cigars. He was supposed to quit, because of his heart and all, but he'd sneak one every now and then." She laughed softly. "I don't know who he thought he was fooling. The foul things stunk up the entire house." Fresh tears welled and she batted her hand in his direction. "I'm sorry," she murmured. "I just can't seem to stop crying."

"Losing somebody you care for is tough. Sometimes it helps to talk about it," he offered slowly, thinking that he might learn more about her relationship with his grandfather.

Gayla lifted her head, her cheeks wet with tears, to peer at him in surprise. His offer was as unexpected as his appearance at Parker House earlier that night. She found nothing but sincerity in his blue eyes, and a warmth that pulled at her, teasing her with the promise of much-needed comfort.

Although tempted beyond words to pour out her worries on this man's shoulders, he was a stranger and a guest. "Thanks, but I'll be fine," she murmured, averting her gaze. She stood and swiped the backs of her hands beneath her cheeks. "Would you like a cup of coffee? I made a fresh pot a little while ago."

Coffee? Damn, the caffeine would keep him up all night, Brett knew, but he could see by the hopeful look on her face that she wasn't wanting to be alone just yet. He found himself unwinding his long legs to stand beside her. "No coffee for me, but a glass of milk sounds mighty good."

"A glass of milk it will be, then, Mr. Sinclair," she said as she turned for the kitchen.

He caught her before she took a full step. "The name's Brett," he said firmly as he guided her back to the chair. "You stay here and keep warm. I'll get our drinks."

"But you're a guest," she objected, her voice rising in panic. "I can't ask you to wait on me."

"You didn't ask, I offered. Now sit right there until I get back."

In the kitchen, as she'd promised, a pot of fresh coffee sat on the stove. Brett quickly poured her a cup, then filled a glass with milk for himself and headed back to the study. She sat where he'd left her, staring at the fire. He thrust the coffee mug under her nose.

Startled, she lifted her gaze. In the firelight he could see that her cheeks were wet, her eyes red and swollen from her crying. He'd never felt more useless in his life.

More gently, he nudged the mug against her hand. She accepted it, slipping two fingers through the curved handle and wrapping both hands around its warmth. "Thank you," she said softly.

"You're welcome." He eased back down beside her and lifted the glass of milk to his lips. When he'd drained the glass, he set it aside. He swiped the back of his hand across his mouth before leaning back with his elbows braced against the carpet and his legs stretched out in front of him.

From the corner of his eye, he watched her. She sat with the mug cradled in her hands, her gaze fixed on the fire, staring, but seeing...what? he wondered. What did she see in the flames? Memories? Regrets, maybe? The sadness, he could understand. But underneath he swore he glimpsed fear. Fear of what? he wondered. Of being alone? Of losing her home, her job?

A stab of guilt made him frown. He wasn't responsible, he told himself as he rubbed his hand across the burning sensation in his stomach. Not for Gayla Matthews. She'd made her own decisions that had brought her to this point, decisions that he'd had no part in. No, he wouldn't feel guilty when Parker House was turned over to the city and she lost her job and her home.

For some reason, telling himself this didn't ease the burning in his stomach any more than the milk.

Gayla closed her eyes and pressed the coffee mug to her forehead to ease the painful throbbing in her head. Catching the movement out of the corner of his eye, Brett turned to her. "Would you like another cup of coffee?"

For a moment Gayla had forgotten Brett still sat beside her. She lowered the cup to her knee, shaking her head. "No, I don't think so."

Brett noticed the trembling in her hand and eased the cup from her grasp and set it aside. "Can I get you anything? An aspirin or something?"

Again she shook her head, even though that simple action was enough to make her head throb even worse. She sank back against the cushions and closed her eyes, smoothing her palms up and down the chair's arms, seeking comfort in the worn leather. She could feel Brett's gaze on her, and even though he was a stranger, she was grateful for his company. "Talk to me," she requested softly. "Please, just talk to me."

Brett looked at her in puzzlement. "About what?"

"Anything. Your life. Your job. What brings you to Braesburg. Anything."

Brett pulled himself from his reclining position and draped his wrists over his knees. "I'm here on business," he finally said and knew it wasn't a lie. He *was* in Braesburg on business—of sorts. "My home is in Kansas City." He stopped, unsure what else to say that wouldn't reveal his identity.

"Do you have family there?" she asked, encouraging him to go on.

"No. Both my parents are dead."

"Any brothers or sisters?"

"No. I was an only child."

"I have nine. Four brothers and five sisters."

Brett whipped his head around to look at her. Her eyes were still closed but a soft, wistful smile curved her lips.

"Nine?" he repeated, unable to believe what she'd said.

"Yes, nine. I haven't seen them in years. They're scattered all over the United States. I'm the only one who remained in Texas."

"Nine," he repeated again as he turned back to the fire, wondering what it would be like to grow up with brothers and sisters. His friends had always considered him lucky, not having to put up with annoying siblings, not having to share toys or the attention of his parents. Of course, they hadn't known what a living hell his home life had been. He'd often wished for brothers or sisters, anyone to detract from the hate that filled his parents' home, but never more than now. If he'd been blessed with siblings, then perhaps he wouldn't have to carry alone the load of family responsibilities that currently weighed so heavily on him.

"What do you do in Kansas City?"

Her question pulled him from his wishful thoughts. "I'm president of Sinclair Corporation, a chain of department stores that my dad owned."

"Hmm. Sounds important. I'm impressed."

Brett scowled at the fire, thinking of the frustrations he dealt with daily. "Don't be. I'm president in title only. The board of directors of the corporation sees to that."

"And that frustrates you," she said knowingly, hearing the level of it in his voice.

"Damn right," he muttered.

She laughed softly. "If I'd been guessing, I'd have guessed you to be a rancher, not a corporate president."

"A rancher?" he echoed, finding himself amused by her assumption. "Why?"

"The jeans, the boots, the truck. Those are more the trappings of a rancher than a corporate executive."

Brett couldn't help but laugh. "My board of directors would probably agree with you. They're always harping at me to improve my image. They'd prefer I wore starched shirts and three-piece suits." He wagged his head regretfully. "Unfortunately, that's not my style. I'm more comfortable in jeans and boots."

"Ned was that way," Gayla replied thoughtfully. "Always thumbing his nose at convention."

Brett frowned at the comparison.

"He caught a lot of flak from the people of the town when he brought me here. There was quite a bit of gossip."

And no wonder! Brett agreed silently. *An old man taking in a young girl more than half his age? Yeah, there was plenty of room for gossip in that arrangement.*

His grandfather's relationship with Gayla was really no concern of his—or so Brett tried to tell himself. But for some reason, he couldn't seem to shake the need to know if she was really in fact the old man's mistress. "Did it bother you?" he asked, unable to suppress his curiosity.

"Some." She smiled sadly, remembering. "But I was accustomed to being the topic of town gossip. Ned, he didn't give a darn what they thought. Once a group of concerned citizens came here and lectured him on appearances and his moral responsibilities as a leader in the community. He told them they could all go to hell."

Good for him, Brett applauded silently, then quickly squelched the traitorous thought. He wouldn't think kind thoughts of the man who had made his own mother's life a living hell.

"So you weren't his mistress?" he asked, unable to contain his curiosity any longer.

Slowly she turned her gaze on him. That he'd insulted her was obvious in the lift of her chin, the ice that chilled her reply. "No, but it certainly didn't stop the talk."

Brett felt a stab of regret for the callous question, but knew it was too late to take it back. Hoping to change the subject to a less invasive one, he asked, "How did you end up as innkeeper at Parker House?"

Gayla's chest rose and fell in a deep, shuddering

breath. She turned her gaze back to the fire. "It's a long story."

Brett lifted his hands. "I'm not going anywhere."

She stared at the fire in silence for so long, Brett decided that she wasn't going to answer his question. When she finally spoke, her voice was barely a whisper. "My family moved around a lot when I was growing up. There were so many of us, and Mother, well, she had a knack for picking the most worthless men for husbands. Each time she married, she promised us that this man would take care of us, that we'd have a home and food and clothes. But they usually ended up taking more than they gave. Wherever we lived, Mother would usually get a job as a waitress or a cook, but with so many of us, what she made was never enough. So we pretty much depended on the kindness and generosity of the townspeople where we lived for our needs. At least we did until we'd worn out our welcome and they ran us out of town."

Brett heard the embarrassment in her voice, the humiliation, but more, he heard the pride that made accepting charity difficult for Gayla.

"Just before school started, my senior year," she continued, "we moved to Braesburg and I got a job as a clerk in Ned's hardware store downtown. Things were going great for us. Mother had married again, husband number six, and we had a little house on the edge of town within walking distance of the schools. But then her husband got laid off and we had to move again. I didn't want to go. I wanted to finish the school year and graduate from Braesburg High.

"Ned knew how much I hated moving, so he went to my mother and stepfather and asked if they'd make Ned legal guardian for me, and allow me to live in the carriage house here at Parker House until school was out."

Brett frowned, thinking of his mother. The old man had kicked out his own daughter, but taken in Gayla, a stranger. The irony of that didn't escape him. "And they agreed?"

"Yes. I was just one less mouth to feed."

Brett could see that Gayla held no ill feelings about the arrangement. "But that was years ago and you're still here."

"Yes, I know. After I finished school, I didn't want to leave. I loved it here. Mr. Parker offered me a full-time job and I worked for him for about three more years. Then he got sick and had to close the store. I couldn't leave then—not when he didn't have anyone to look after him—so I stayed on as his housekeeper and nurse."

"For the same salary, I hope."

She shook her head. "I wouldn't accept his money. After all, he provided me a home and never asked anything of me in return."

Brett couldn't decide if she was that foolish or that kind, but either way he figured Ned had come out ahead. "What about the bed-and-breakfast? How did that come about?"

"Need. Mr. Parker's business had been on the decline for years before he was forced by his health to close it down. Bills had stacked up and he was having a hard time making ends meet."

"Why didn't he just sell the place?"

"Mr. Parker would never sell Parker House," she said adamantly. "Turning it into a bed-and-breakfast offered us income without sacrificing the house."

Brett snorted. "Stubborn old cuss, if you ask me. He should have sold the property."

"Yes, he was stubborn, all right. But Parker House meant more to him than the money it would bring. It was his home. And in a way, mine, too."

To Brett's way of thinking, Ned Parker was a fool, and Gayla a bigger one for going along with him. He turned to tell her just that, but stopped when he saw the glimmer of tears in her eyes. As he watched, the tears brimmed over her eyelids and streaked down her face.

"I'm sorry," he said, ashamed that he'd made her cry again. He lifted a hand to cover hers. "I didn't mean to upset you." Heat from her hand seeped through his fingers, setting every nerve ending in his body to pulsing. Quickly, he snatched his hand back.

Unaware of the effect she had on him, she shook her head. "No. What you said is true. Ned Parker was a stubborn old cuss. But I loved him," she said, her voice hitching. She turned to face Brett fully, tears streaming down her face. "He offered me what I'd always dreamed of. A home. Family and roots. And now he's gone."

Her tears grew in intensity until her shoulders racked with heartbreaking sobs. Brett felt wholly responsible, for he was the one who'd dredged up the memories by delving into her past. He knelt in front of her chair, but he kept his hands glued to his thighs, reluctant to touch her again.

"Gayla, I'm sorry," he said, for those were the only words of comfort he knew to offer. A wisp of hair blocked his view of her face. Careful not to touch her, he caught it and tucked it behind her ear. "Please, don't cry," he begged her.

Brett couldn't stand the sight of her suffering any longer. He wrapped an arm around her and pulled her against his chest. His eyes widened in surprise when, on a broken sob, she threw her arms around his neck and buried her face against his cheek. She clung to him like he was a life raft in a storm-tossed sea. Unsure what to do, he self-consciously rubbed a hand up and down her back, trying to calm her.

"Shh," he soothed, his cheek moving against her hair. The silky tresses whispered against his unshaven cheek, unleashing the scent of roses. The combination of silk and roses was irresistible. He buried his nose deeper into her hair, filling his senses with the intoxicating fragrance. "Please, don't cry anymore," he murmured softly.

But her sobbing continued, growing in depth and intensity. She felt so small in his arms, so fragile. He knew she didn't deserve this misery, any more than his mother had deserved what she'd suffered at the hand of Ned Parker. An unexpected need to protect Gayla welled within him. He gathered her closer, slowly rocking her back and forth.

She tightened her arms around him, and the swell of her breasts pressed seductively against his chest. His body responded in the most elemental way. Heat curled lazily in his groin, then surged upward to spread through his chest. His breath came in increasingly shorter bursts, stirring her hair.

He turned his lips to her temple. It was only a natural progression to her cheek. Her skin was soft beneath his lips, and flavored with the salt of her tears. Needing to see her, to anchor himself both emotionally and physically, he caught her chin in his hand and tipped her face up to his.

Her gaze met his—brown eyes flooded with tears, appearing like circles of molten chocolate against her pale skin. The utter hopelessness in her expression stabbed at his heart. So young, he thought sadly, to have the weight of the world heaped on her shoulders. All she'd done was care for an old man, and in doing so, had seemingly sacrificed her youth and her future.

She shouldn't have looked desirable to him at that moment, with her eyes all red and puffy and her cheeks wet with tears, dressed in a tattered blue terry robe. Yet, she did. More desirable than anyone he'd met in a long time.

Full and moist, her lips were slightly parted and a breath away from his own, tempting him to draw closer. Without thinking of anything beyond the moment, he lowered his head.

The warmth of his breath touched Gayla first, followed quickly by the searing heat of his lips on hers. At the initial contact, she stiffened, then slowly she let herself go, melting into him, accepting his kiss, drawing from it.

He offered an easy path from grief to passion, one Gayla navigated without even realizing she'd made the step.

She needed his warmth, his comfort, the distraction from her grief, her worries. She clung to him, desperately absorbing the strength he offered so willingly, needing to feel the thrum of youth and vitality that pumped through his veins and the life that warmed her hands. The touch of his lips on hers was tender and giving. The shared breath, a renewal of life she needed in order to go on.

His arms tightened around her, the muscles in his back bunching and shifting beneath her hands, and their intimacy climbed to another level. She clawed at him, her nails digging into his back, flesh against flesh, heat drawing heat.

Her actions incited Brett, fanning the flames that already heated his blood to near boiling. He drew her closer still, until he'd dragged her from the chair and she lay sprawled across his knees, her face turned up to his, allowing him easier access to her lips. With her crushed against his chest, his lips on hers, he tugged the afghan free of her legs and tossed it in front of the fire. He followed, carrying her with him, gently laying her in front of the fire, then dragging his lips down the smooth column of her neck to the skin exposed in the veed opening formed by her robe's collar. He soothed her not with words, but with his hands and his mouth, kissing away the salty tears, lighting fires where the chill of grief had threatened before.

Before he realized what was happening, he'd nudged the panels of her robe farther apart, exposing more and more skin for his ministrations until he'd bared a breast. Bathed a rosy hue by the glow of the fire, the delicate translucency of her skin lured him on. He touched a finger to the budded nipple that had taunted him through the thin robe, and felt the shudder of desire course through her. On a groan, he closed his mouth over the pebbled orb, drawing it deep within his mouth. Gayla arched beneath him, framing his face to hold him close.

Desire became something fierce, threatening to consume them if not sated. Moving quickly, Brett caught the tie of her robe and yanked it free, pushing the folds of her robe away. Shucking out of his jeans, he angled himself between her legs. His gaze locked on her face, slowly, rhythmically, he rubbed his groin against the pillowed softness of her femininity, teasing her, taunting her until her chest heaved and her breath came in ragged gasps.

"Oh, God, please," she whispered, begging for release.

He rose above her, sliding his hands down her back until her buttocks rested in the breadth of his hands. He lifted, his own breath rasping, and guided her to him.

Her breath caught at the joining, and then escaped in a low, guttural moan as he moved inside her, carrying her farther and farther away from the sadness, the grief, the fears.

She slept like an angel.

Brett lay beside Gayla, watching her, his head propped on his bent arm, his elbow buried in the tangled folds of her robe. With a gentleness that was totally uncharacteristic of him, he caught a wisp of blond hair and tucked it behind her ear to better see her face. Her features were well-defined, patrician almost in their design, yet totally and undeniably feminine. He traced the lines, beginning at her forehead, trailing down her nose, across the slash of cheekbone to the delicate curve of her ear.

His chest rose and fell in a deep sigh as he let his palm cradle the elegant contour of her jaw. He'd never felt so…so soft toward a woman before, almost as if his heart had melted in his chest. How had this happened? he wondered again. How had his offer of comfort to this woman turned into the wild play of lovemaking that had resulted?

He brushed a knuckle along the thick curl of lashes that fanned beneath her eyes. At the moment, he didn't care what had transpired. He was too weak, too sated to care much about anything.

A shiver shook him and he cut a glance at the dying embers in the fireplace. Not knowing where more firewood was stored, he heaved a resigned sigh. If he didn't get them to a bed and under some covers, they were liable to both catch their death of cold. Pushing to his feet, he pulled on his jeans, then carefully tucked Gayla's robe around her shoulders.

Kneeling, he gathered her into his arms, then stood. Moaning softly, she nestled against him, seeking the warmth of his chest, but her eyes remained closed, her sleep undisturbed.

His heart swelled at her unconscious seeking of him as her fingers curled into a soft fist against his chest. Smiling tenderly down at Gayla, Brett carried her up the stairs to his room.

Gayla awakened with a start, her heart hammering in her chest. Disoriented, she pushed to her elbows, and the bedcovers slipped to her waist. *Mrs. Parker's room?* she wondered in confusion. What was she doing here? Suddenly chilled, she looked down and was shocked to find herself naked. A movement beside her made her whip her head around. Brett lay on the bed at her side, groping for the covers she'd robbed from him when she'd bolted upright.

Although she had no memory of coming to this room, the events of the previous night came rushing back.

"Oh, my God," she whispered against trembling fingers. "What have I done?"

Inching carefully to the edge of the mattress, she slipped from beneath the covers and grabbed her robe from the foot of the bed where Brett must have draped it after carrying her to his room. Ramming her arms through the sleeves, she yanked the belt tight around her waist and all but ran to the door. Opening it slowly, she slipped through the narrow opening and closed it softly behind her. Once free of the room, she collapsed against the wall and covered her mouth with trembling hands.

How will I ever be able to face him in the morning? she wailed inwardly.

Three

Brett rolled onto his back, stretching his hands to the headboard and his toes to the foot of the bed. With a growl and a shudder, he sank back against the pillow and reached for Gayla. His hands came up with only air. Opening one eye, he lifted his head and cut a glance to the other side of the bed and found it empty. Her absence both angered and saddened him.

He dropped his head back onto the pillow and covered his face with his hands. *You fool, you fool, you fool,* he cursed himself inwardly, as he dragged his hands roughly down his face. *What were you thinking!*

He tried to convince himself that she was as guilty as he, for he certainly hadn't forced her—but he knew that was only half the truth. She couldn't be held responsible for her actions. He'd taken advantage of her grief-stricken state. He'd played on her vulnerability, taken what she'd so innocently offered, and given her— What? he demanded of himself. What had he given her in return?

Nothing, he told himself, but a momentary escape from her misery. And to add insult to injury, now he was about to strip her of her home.

But he could give her one thing, he told himself as he levered himself from the bed. He would save her the embarrassment of having to face him in the light of day. He would take a quick shower, pack his bag and slip out before she knew he was gone. He could grab some breakfast at the diner he'd eaten at the day before, put in a call to his grandfather's attorney, take care of the legalities of settling the estate, and get out of town.

He strode to the window and pushed back the drapes. Sun glistened off the trees' ice-covered branches, already melting away winter's ravages of the night before. But he knew bad weather wouldn't have stopped him from doing what he had to do. Nothing could.

Gayla stood in the doorway to the room where Brett had slept, one hand braced against the doorjamb to keep herself from succumbing to the dizzying sensation that dragged at her. The bedcoverings hung crazily from one side of the bed. His duffel bag was gone, as were the clothes and boots she'd stepped over as she'd stolen from his room in the middle of the night. The bathroom door stood ajar, allowing scents of soap and a manly after-shave to mingle with the fragrance of the lavender potpourri she kept in a crystal bowl on the dresser.

That he was gone was obvious.

She'd suspected as much when he hadn't responded to her call for breakfast, had even prayed he had left so that she wouldn't have to face him after what had happened the night before. But the proof of his hasty departure saddened her in a way she couldn't explain.

She entered the room slowly, stooping to pick up a damp towel from the floor. She drew it to her face, inhaling the scent of him as she crossed to the bed. Tears of regret burned her eyes as she accepted the fact that he was gone and she would never see him again. In leaving, he took with him any hope that Gayla might secretly have harbored for a second taste of their passion.

Her fingertips trailed the high, polished footboard, remembering the comfort, the passion she'd experienced in his arms, knowing that in the lonely nights to come, she would resurrect that memory and draw comfort from it again.

With a sigh, she scooped up the bedspread and tangle of blankets and tossed them back across the bed. A flutter of paper on the pillow caught her eye and she froze as she stared at the crisp bills that settled in the dent on the pillow left by Brett's head. Two one-hundred-dollar bills. More than twice the price she'd named for the room. Humiliation seared her cheeks and burned through her chest as she realized he'd left the money for more than the cost of his lodging.

He was paying for services rendered by the innkeeper of Parker House.

Brett dropped a quarter in the slot and dialed the number he'd scrawled on the back of a business card. "I need to speak with John Thomas, please," he told the receptionist who answered the phone.

"May I ask who's calling?"

"Brett Sinclair."

"Just a moment, please."

He didn't have to wait long before a man's voice came across the line.

"John Thomas. May I help you?"

"I hope so. My name's Brett Sinclair. I'm Christine Parker Sinclair's son."

There was a pregnant pause, then the lawyer said dryly, "I had hoped to hear from Christine, herself."

Brett could hear the censure in the man's voice, and fought down the anger it spawned. "I'm calling on her behalf."

"She couldn't trouble herself to make the call personally?"

"Christine Sinclair died six months ago," Brett replied impatiently. "As her son and only living heir, I'm the executor of her estate."

"I see." There was another pause. "So that would make you sole heir to your grandfather's property, as well?"

"Yeah, it looks that way. I was hoping we could set up an appointment to get this mess taken care of."

"The sooner the better."

"I'm calling from a pay phone at the diner on Main Street. I can be at your office in ten minutes, if it's convenient."

"Fine. I'll have the will ready."

Located on the second floor of Braesburg's only bank, John Thomas's office further substantiated Brett's suspicions that he was dealing with a small-time lawyer. A single door marked the entrance while black lettering in a simple style spelled out John Thomas, Attorney-at-Law on the smoked glass. Nothing like the suite of offices his mother's attorney manned in downtown Kansas City where dark oak and plush carpeting dominated.

John Thomas himself—an imposing man in both stature and manner—greeted Brett at the door. The two men sized each other up for a tense moment before John stretched out a hand. "John Thomas," he said by way of introduction. "I was your grandfather's attorney."

"Brett Sinclair." Brett gave the offered hand a firm shake, then quickly released it.

John gestured toward his office. "I have the legal documents ready. Would you like a cup of coffee?"

Brett unconsciously touched his hand to his stomach, where the burning had returned with a vengeance. "No, thanks."

With a whatever-you-say shrug, John led the way

into his office. "Your grandfather was a stickler for detail and kept his will current. As a personal friend of Ned's, I can assure you that he was in a sound mental state at the time of the last modification."

Brett slouched in the chair and propped an elbow on the chair's arm. Doubtful of the old man's mental state no matter what his age, he rubbed a finger above his upper lip and murmured dryly, "I'll take your word for it."

By the disapproving arch of the lawyer's eyebrow, Brett could see that John didn't care for his sarcasm. "Let's get on with it," he said impatiently.

"We will have the reading as soon—" The lawyer glanced up, stopping mid-sentence when the office door opened. He rose, smiling. "Gayla. I was afraid the road conditions might delay you."

Brett whipped his head around, sure that he had misunderstood John. But Gayla stood in the doorway, her gaze frozen on Brett. He watched as the blood slowly drained from her face.

Slowly Brett rose to his feet.

John moved around his desk to make the necessary introductions. "Gayla, I'd like you to meet Brett Sinclair, Ned's grandson. Brett, this is Gayla Matthews, Ned's devoted companion and friend."

They stood for a moment, staring. Gayla's face was pale and tense, Brett's flushed in anger. He'd tried to avoid this encounter. He'd wanted to save her the embarrassment of having to face him after what had transpired the night before, knowing she would regret her actions in the light of day, but thanks to John Thomas, his efforts were for naught.

Dipping her chin to her chest and averting her gaze, Gayla brushed by Brett and took the other chair that faced John's desk.

Brett remained standing. ''Is her presence necessary?'' he asked with a jerk of his head in Gayla's direction.

''She's here at Ned's request.''

There was no way John could know the reason behind the tension between him and Gayla, but that the man was aware of it, Brett was sure.

''If you'll be seated, we'll begin,'' John instructed.

Slowly, Brett dropped back down in the chair as John smoothed an age-spotted hand down the typed documents and began to read. Brett listened impatiently through the standard legal mumbo jumbo, wishing there was some way to escape this hellhole he'd managed to create. He didn't dare look at Gayla, but he was fully aware of her presence. Anger emanated from her like the cloying fragrance of a cheap perfume. And it was justified. After all, he was sure she believed she'd slept with the enemy. He should have told her from the first that he was Ned's grandson instead of allowing John to drop the bomb on her so unexpectedly. But it was too late for regrets. The best he could do would be to end this as quickly as possible.

'''All real estate, and other assets, I bequeath to my daughter, Christine.'''

The clause was the escape hole Brett had been waiting for. He bolted to his feet, anxious to put an end to Gayla's misery. "As Christine Parker Sinclair's heir, I would like to donate the entire estate to the city of Braesburg."

Beside him, Gayla sucked in a shocked breath. John leveled him with a chilling glare. "That's very generous of you, Mr. Sinclair, but before the estate can be disposed of, there are certain requirements that must be fulfilled."

"Like what?" Brett demanded impatiently.

"Liens, to begin with," John said. "But there are other contingencies as well, which Ned clearly defines in the will. If you'll allow me to continue."

Feeling like a schoolboy who'd had his knuckles rapped by his teacher, Brett sat back down, scowling.

"'Before Christine or her heirs can claim the estate,'" John continued reading, "'she/they must reside at Parker House for a term of no less than six months.'"

Brett's chest tightened in anger.

"'At that time, she/they are free to dispose of any portion of the estate that is deemed necessary with the exception of Parker House, which is further explained in Section III, paragraph five of this document.'"

John carefully turned the page. "The next portion of the will deals specifically with you, Gayla," he said, sending a sympathetic smile her way. "The words are Ned's, written in his own hand." He paused to clear his throat. "'To Gayla Matthews'" he read solemnly, "'I leave my heartfelt thanks for her unfailing care and affection. You've been like a daughter to me, Gayla, loving and kind in your care for me, and totally selfless. Until which time you choose to marry or until your death, Parker House is to be your home. Because you love it as I do, I feel that this is the greatest gift I can give you.'''

Brett couldn't believe what he was hearing. He twisted around to look at Gayla, sure that she must have been privy to this information. But although her lower lip quivered and her eyes glistened with tears, she appeared as shocked as he was by the news. He jerked his gaze to John Thomas. ''He can't do this!'' he roared angrily.

''He not only can, he did.'' John reared back in his chair and leveled Brett with a cold stare. ''And I assure you, it is all within the limits of the law.''

Brett dropped his elbows to his knees and his forehead to his palms, trying to think of a way out of the conflicting stipulations. ''Let me see if I understand this,'' he said after a moment, as he slowly lifted his head, dragging his fingers through his hair. ''Before I can dispose of the estate, I must pay off all the liens against it, live at Parker House for six months, and even then I can't get rid of the house as long as Gayla is alive?''

''Or until she marries,'' John clarified. ''In which case all stipulations of the testament will have been satisfied.'' John shuffled through the papers, then pushed a page across the desk to Brett. ''Parker House is only a portion of the estate. Appendix A is a complete list of all Ned's assets.'' He laid a manila envelope on top of the single sheet. ''Here is your copy of the will.'' He placed an identical file in front of Gayla, his expression softening when he looked her way. ''Do either of you have any questions?''

Gayla shook her head.

Brett remained silent. Even from the grave, it seemed the old man would still have the last word.

Still feeling raw and exposed after the confrontation with Brett in John's office, Gayla dragged her arms from her coat sleeves, then hung it on one of the pegs by the back entry of Parker House. She should have known, she told herself miserably as she stepped into the kitchen and tied an apron around her waist. She should have recognized the similarities that now seemed so obvious.

Brett Sinclair was enough like his grandfather to be his son.

She hadn't known Ned in his younger days, but she suspected that he must have looked a lot like Brett then. They shared the same build: tall, broad shoulders, narrow hips and long legs. Even their eyes were the same unique shade of blue, although the years had dimmed the intensity in Ned's.

Needing the mindless activity of performing an everyday task, she pulled the flour canister from the pantry, then reached for the shortening. She'd seen glimpses during her conversations with Brett of the same stubbornness that Ned had worn like a shield, the same gruffness he'd used to hide a tender heart.

He even smiled like Ned, she remembered with a measure of resentment, one corner of his mouth tipped up just a little higher than the other, as if he didn't deserve the happiness a full smile reflected. She'd always assumed the loss of his family was what had robbed Ned of any pleasure he might have found in life and had left him a bitter old man. But what about Brett? What had happened to him?

Her thoughts drifted further, remembering Brett's anger as he'd stalked from John's office and the squeal of his tires as he'd driven away without a word of explanation to either of them. What bitterness fed his fury? What had spawned the hate that made him determined to see the demise of Parker House? He'd inherited a sizable estate, but was willing to give it all to the city of Braesburg. Why?

She remembered the crisp bills lying on the pillow and felt tears building in her eyes, humiliated that he'd thought he could pay her like she was some whore. She swiped furiously at the tears before sinking her hands into the pastry dough. It didn't matter, she told herself. People had thought less of her and she'd survived. She certainly wouldn't lose any sleep over Brett Sinclair's opinion.

Brett was tempted to head his truck for Kansas City and forget he'd ever heard of Ned Parker, or Parker House, or Gayla Matthews. He'd even driven an hour in that direction before his sense of duty and responsibility had overridden his anger and he'd turned around and started back.

He would never admit that Gayla had played a part in that decision to return. But she had. He couldn't forget the look on her face when she'd walked into John Thomas's office and seen him sitting there. Shock had been her first response, freezing her to that spot of carpet and stripping her face of color. He could understand the shock and accepted total responsibility for it, for it was his own fault she hadn't known his connection to Ned Parker. But he could have lived with that bit of guilt.

The part that haunted him, the part he couldn't excuse, was what had followed her initial jolt of recognition. The shame. It had painted high points of color on her cheeks and shadowed her eyes. That was his fault, as well. And he was too much of a gentleman to be able to live with that measure of guilt.

He remembered, too, how fragile she'd felt in his arms, how incredibly sweet and innocent. How she'd looked when she slept—like an angel. And he would never forget what had happened between those two memories; the passion that burned within her, a passion that struck like a flash point. He'd never in his life felt so emotionally bared—a dangerous position for a man who guarded his emotions the way most men guarded their wealth.

Quickly, he pushed aside those thoughts and focused on what he needed to do to set things right.

He knew he couldn't roll back the clock and erase what had happened between them, but he could possibly improve her chances for a more solid future. He would go back to Braesburg, he'd finally decided, fulfill the requirements of the old man's will, donate Parker House to the city, dissolve the remaining assets of the estate and give Gayla whatever money it generated. He didn't need it, didn't want it, but he suspected that Gayla did. And she deserved whatever happiness it would bring.

He knew he couldn't tell her of his plans to give her the money generated from Ned's estate. He knew she would never accept a penny from him. Not now. Not after what had happened between them. He would simply instruct John Thomas to give it to her once he'd taken care of everything and left town.

Brett spent the return trip studying his options and laying out a plan. Once he pulled into the driveway and stepped from his truck, all that remained was for him to convince Gayla to go along with his plan. And he knew that was easier said than done.

He found her in the kitchen, as he'd expected, working. Startled by the opening of the back door, she whirled when he stepped inside. When she saw him, she quickly turned back to her cutting board, her cheeks flaming, her eyes downcast, and continued to knead the dough.

"We need to talk," he said gruffly and whipped out a chair from the kitchen table.

"All right," she replied, although she kept her back to him and her hands buried in the dough.

He watched her in growing frustration, her reluctance to face him fostering his own sense of guilt. "Could you at least sit down for a minute, so we can do this face-to-face?"

Without a word, Gayla dropped the dough and scraped the clinging pastry from her fingers. She shifted to the sink, washed her hands, then moved to the table and the chair opposite his as she dried them, all the while managing to avoid meeting his gaze.

Before she sat down, she dipped her hand into the pocket of her apron and withdrew a crumpled wad of bills, which she tossed onto the table in front of him. She sat then, and looked him squarely in the eyes, her chin cocked at a proud angle. His heart sank as he realized that she'd mistaken the payment for more than the costs of a night's lodging.

He pushed the bills back across the table. "I left this to cover the price of the room," he mumbled.

She shoved it right back. "I can't very well charge the owner for something that is rightfully his."

Although he wanted to argue the point, Brett scraped the money off the table and stuffed it into his shirt pocket.

"About the will," he began, anxious to get this confrontation behind him.

Gayla lifted a hand to interrupt him. "First, I'd like to ask you something."

Although he feared her question might concern the intimacy they'd shared, Brett muttered a reluctant, "Okay."

"Why didn't you tell me you were Ned's grandson?"

The question, if possible, was just as difficult to answer as the one he'd expected. "I don't know," he answered honestly. "I don't even know what possessed me to come here in the first place. My intention was to settle my grandfather's estate and get out of town as quickly as possible. But when I was driving down Main Street looking for a place to spend the night, I saw the street sign for Oak Knoll and couldn't resist driving by the place.

"Before I even realized what I was doing, I was standing on the porch, ringing the bell. Once you opened the door, I didn't know what to do but ask for a room. When I registered and you didn't seem to recognize my name, I decided to keep my relationship to Ned to myself. It seemed wiser that way."

Her face deepened in color. "You let me talk about him, you asked questions about his family, you even pried into my own personal life, yet you thought it wise to keep *your* identity a secret?"

He shrugged self-consciously, knowing her anger was justified. "At the time, it made sense."

"Well, it doesn't make sense to me!" she retorted. "When I think of the things I told you, the way I accepted your comfort, of what we did—" She covered her face with her hands, obviously humiliated by the memory.

Brett didn't have a clue what to say to make her feel better. So he sat, too, and waited. After a few moments, she dragged her hands from her face to clasp them on the tabletop. She lifted her chin at the same angle he'd witnessed at the cemetery, and he wondered again if it was pride or defiance behind it.

"What did you want to talk to me about?" she asked coolly.

"The future," he said hesitantly, unsure how she would respond to his idea. "In order to meet the stipulations of the will, I'm prepared to pay off the liens currently held on this property. The six-month residency requirement will be an inconvenience, at best, but I'm willing to fulfill that obligation, as well. I'll move in here, and run my business long distance for the required six months. The last contingency, though, I don't have any power over.'' He scooped the saltshaker from the table and rolled it between his hands, preferring to look at it rather than Gayla when he posed his next question. ''I don't suppose you have a fiancé or a boyfriend hanging around waiting to marry you?''

Gayla stared at the top of his head, unable to believe he was asking such a thing, especially after what had happened between them. ''No, and my health is excellent, in case you're wondering,'' she replied, not even attempting to disguise the bitterness in her voice.

Brett let out a heavy sigh and set the saltshaker aside. ''As far as I can see, then, there is only one option left for us.''

His air of resignation made Gayla suddenly wary. ''And what would that be?'' she asked.

''We'll get married.''

She bolted to her feet. ''We'll, *what?*'' she cried in disbelief.

''We'll get married,'' he repeated. ''It'll be a marriage in name only,'' he added in case she thought he was offering anything more. He didn't want her assuming anything different, for he had no intention of marrying Gayla, or any other woman for that matter, in the true sense of the word. He hadn't reached the age of thirty as a bachelor by accident. It had been a choice. A necessary one. ''After my six months are up, we'll file for a divorce. That way, I can legally dispose of the estate and we can both get on with our lives.''

''Parker House *is* my life,'' she countered, curling her hands into fists on the tabletop.

''I know it was in the past,'' he replied reasonably. ''But there's no reason for you to feel obligated to stay on here any longer. Ned's dead, Gayla,'' he said patiently. ''You don't have to take care of him or support him anymore.''

Moisture flooded her eyes. ''You'd give Parker House away?'' she whispered, still unable to believe he would do such a thing.

Brett shrugged. ''It means nothing to me.''

''But it did to Ned!'' she retorted. ''He loved this house, and sacrificed everything to keep it for his family.''

''He kept it for his family?'' Brett laughed, although the sound lacked any trace of humor. ''If he wanted to keep it for his family, why did he kick my mother out when she was nineteen? And if he supposedly cared so much for his family, why didn't he ever contact his daughter or come around? Ned Parker may have loved this house,'' he said, leveling a finger at her nose, ''but he didn't give a damn about his family. He was stingy and mean and stubborn—''

Gayla slapped his hand from beneath her nose. ''Don't you dare speak about Ned that way in this house.''

Brett rocked his chair back on two legs and hooked his thumbs over his belt, eyeing her lazily. "Kind of taking a lot for granted, aren't you? He didn't *leave* the house to you—only the right of residency."

"I'm not pretending to own the house, Mr. Sinclair. Only defending a man who isn't here to defend himself."

Angry silence stretched between the two as they continued to glare at each other in a silent battle of wills. It was Brett who finally broke the silence. "You haven't answered my question, yet," he said, and lowered the chair to all four legs. "Will you marry me?"

"So that you can fulfill the requirements of Ned's will and destroy Parker House?" She didn't wait for an answer. She didn't need one. Brett had made his plans for his inheritance quite clear. "Why should I?" she demanded angrily. "Ned gave me the right to residency. You need me," she said, tapping a finger at her chest. "I certainly don't need you."

"Oh, don't you?" Brett demanded, his own temper rising. "And how do you plan to maintain the place? Upkeep alone will eat you alive."

"With profits from the bed-and-breakfast."

"You seem to forget that *I* own the property. *I* decide if the house will be used as a business and, if it is, how the income produced from that business will be spent." He narrowed his gaze menacingly. "And I can assure you, I won't sink another thin dime into this place until you agree to marry me."

He played to win; Gayla could see that in the determined gleam in his eye and the arrogant set of his jaw. She didn't doubt for a minute that he would stand by and watch Parker House crumble to the ground in disrepair. Time was what she needed. Time to think of a way to save Parker House.

"How about a compromise?" Gayla suggested. "After you've completed your six-month residency requirement, I'll marry you."

Brett snorted. "Do I look like a fool?" He shook his head, chuckling. "I'm not wasting six months of my life fulfilling some damn-fool residency requirement without a guarantee that at the end of that six months *all* the requirements will have been met. Now, I'm going to ask you one more time. Will you marry me?"

"And if I don't?"

"Then I'll walk away. I'm sure that at some point in time, whoever holds the liens on the property will confiscate the estate for payment. Then the future of your precious Parker House will become a moot point, won't it?"

Gayla felt as if she were teetering on a finely stretched wire, for she knew why Ned had placed in his will the stipulation of her residency. Granted, he'd wanted to make sure she had a home, but she suspected he'd also wanted to save Parker House. Knowing that she loved the place as much as he, he'd left the responsibility of its future fully in Gayla's hands.

And there was no way in hell that Gayla would ever let Ned down.

She quickly determined that there was only one way to save Parker House, and that was to make Brett care as deeply for the family home as Ned had. But she needed time to accomplish this. She wasn't sure six months was long enough, but that was all the time Ned had allowed her in his will. If she had to marry Brett to keep him at Parker House in order to achieve this, then so be it. She had nowhere else to go, nothing to lose.

"Yes," she whispered. "I'll marry you."

Forty-eight hours, Gayla reflected miserably, staring into the fire from the comfort of Ned's old leather chair. Forty-eight hours to come to terms with the agreement she'd made with Brett and prepare for her marriage.

If possible, her misery deepened. Marriage. She'd never put much thought into the eventuality of marriage or the planning of a wedding, but whatever thoughts she might have fostered had never resembled anything close to this. A convenience, he'd called it, she reflected bitterly. But for whom?

There should be bridesmaids, she thought, her blue mood darkening, and flowers and a church bedecked with greenery and candles. Months of planning, shopping for the perfect dress, selecting silver and china patterns, and bridal luncheons and showers. And love, she added lastly.

She pulled the afghan closer around her shoulders, huddling under its warmth to ward off the room's chill, but also to hold her misery close. At the moment, misery was her only companion.

With Brett's departure for Kansas City to make the

necessary arrangements to continue his business from Parker House and packing what he'd need for the next six months, the house suddenly seemed unusually quiet and empty around her.

And that was ridiculous, she scolded herself. She'd had the house to herself for months after Ned's confinement to the nursing home and she'd never once felt lonely or felt the need for companionship. She'd always been the caretaker, the nurturer, too busy fulfilling the needs of others to realize she had needs of her own that needed filling.

But Brett had changed all that.

Defensively, she tugged the afghan closer. She hadn't wanted his comfort, she told herself, hadn't asked for it. Yet, when it was offered, she'd grabbed at it, clung to it and to him, finding warmth and comfort when her own life seemed filled with despair. Now she'd experienced the release, the freedom obtained in sharing one's burdens. The release of being comforted, instead of always offering comfort. The strength that could be drawn from a comforting word, a simple touch.

A simple touch? she thought with a shiver, remembering. His touch had been anything but simple...and something she feared she would spend a lifetime trying to forget.

"The wedding will take place tomorrow evening at six at Parker House. I'm going to ask Reverend Brown to perform the ceremony, and I want you to be there as our witness." Gayla knotted and unknotted her fingers. "But you are the only one who is to know the truth behind the marriage."

John Thomas's frown deepened. "Don't you think Reverend Brown might be a little suspicious, considering you've only known Sinclair a couple of days?"

Unable to sit any longer, Gayla rose to pace John's office. "Probably, but he's too polite to probe."

"The rest of the town's not. There'll be talk."

Gayla stopped at the window and looked out, folding her arms protectively beneath her breasts. All signs of the ice storm that had hit Braesburg days before were gone. The frost that it had left on her heart remained. "It won't be the first time I've been the topic of town gossip."

John shoved back his chair and stood. "Gayla, you don't have to go through with this."

"Yes, I do, for Ned's sake." She turned and looked at John, her eyes brimming with tears, but with her chin lifted in determination. "If I don't, Brett will walk away and let the property be confiscated by the state. You know how much Ned loved Parker House. I can't stand by and watch that happen."

"Do you really think six months will make a difference to the man? Seems to me that he's already made up his mind about the place."

"I don't know, but it's my only hope." She took John's hand in hers and squeezed. "Please understand, John. I have to try."

Four

The Reverend Mark Brown stood before the fireplace, the same worn Bible he'd used at Ned's funeral spread across his open palms. Off to his right stood John Thomas, his disapproval of the proceedings obvious in the tenseness of his jaw, and his distrust of Brett in his narrowed eyes. Gayla faced them both, her fingers clutched around a simple bouquet of white rosebuds, an unexpected gift from Brett who stood tall and solemn at her side. The thoughtfulness behind the gesture tightened her throat and misted her eyes.

She tried hard not to think about the man beside her, the man she pledged her life to as she repeated the vows. Love, honor, cherish until death us do part. All lies voiced to make their union legal in the eyes of the law.

"The rings, please," the reverend asked, looking inquiringly at first Gayla, then Brett.

Gayla lifted her gaze to Brett, unsure what to say or do. He hesitated only slightly, then, without a word drew the chain from beneath his collar and slipped the gold band from its links. "My grandmother's," he murmured in explanation as he took Gayla's hand in his.

Surprised, Gayla could do nothing but stare while Brett slipped the ring onto her finger, then slowly released her hand, dragging his gaze from hers as he turned once again to face the reverend. With unexpected tears burning her eyes, Gayla curled her fingers into her palm, shocked to find herself wishing with all her heart that the feel of the gold band, still warm from his body, was a sign of more than just a charade.

"I now pronounce you man and wife. You may kiss your bride."

Gayla was sure that Brett would ignore the offer, even prayed he would, but instead he turned to her, gently taking her cheeks between his hands, and lowering his head to hers. Their lips touched briefly and Gayla nearly cried at the familiar warmth and taste of him. When he would have deepened the kiss, though, she pulled back, hiding the emotions she feared would give her heart away.

All business, John Thomas stepped forward. "I'll need both your signatures here on the marriage certificate." He waited while Brett took the pen and scrawled his name, then passed it to Gayla who signed beneath. Reverend Brown signed next, then John

Thomas added his own signature as witness. The lawyer folded the certificate and slipped it into the breast pocket of his suit. "I'll file the certificate at the courthouse. You'll receive your copy by mail."

And then it was over. In a span of ten minutes, Gayla's life had changed forever. Needing to distance herself from Brett, she tucked her arm through Reverend Brown's and walked with him to the entry hall to collect his coat. Brett started to follow, but John Thomas stepped in front of the doorway, blocking his path.

"Braesburg's a small town," John said, keeping his voice low. "News of this little wedding will be served right along with breakfast in the morning at every table in town. If you are any kind of man at all, you'll protect her from more hurt." Having had his say, he stepped aside.

Gayla waited in the foyer, holding John Thomas's coat. As the two men stepped into the foyer, she glanced from Brett to John sensing the tension between them. Without a word, Brett turned away and headed down the hall for the kitchen.

John forced a smile. "Thanks, Gayla," he said, as she helped him into his coat. He caught her hand and squeezed, his eyes filled with concern. "If you need anything, anything at all, promise me you'll give me a call?"

She could only nod. She walked the two men to the door and thanked them again for their services. She watched them walk down the sidewalk, side by side, then split as they each headed for their cars. A part of her wanted to chase after them and beg them to end this charade. But the future of Parker House rested on her compliance with Brett's agreement and she couldn't—wouldn't—let Ned down.

With a heavy sigh, she closed the door and turned to find Brett standing in the hallway behind her, waiting. She stiffened at the sight of him. He'd removed his coat, loosened the top button on his dress shirt and cuffed the sleeves to his elbows. His relaxed appearance was a contrast to her own tense state.

He held a glass of champagne in each hand and extended one toward her. "How about a toast to the new bride and groom?" he asked, teasing her with that half smile that was so much like Ned's.

Gayla simply looked at him, the farce of the ceremony too fresh to be forgotten, amazed that he could joke about something as serious as the vows they'd just made to each other. "If you'll excuse me," she said, brushing past him. "I'm going to my room and lie down."

Gayla lay on her bed in the old maid's quarters off the kitchen, surrounded by darkness, still dressed in the ivory crepe suit she'd worn for her wedding, a quilt pulled to her chin. In the other part of the house she could hear Brett moving around, first in the kitchen—water splashing, glasses clinking—then the sound of his footsteps on the stairs. His room was situated just above hers, and although his movements were muffled, she judged by the sounds filtering through the ceiling that he must be getting ready for bed.

She listened to the thud of first one boot, then the other hitting the floor. She squeezed her eyes shut, trying not to envision him stripping out of his clothes. The images came anyway, filling her mind and making her burn. She remembered too well the strength of his body and how it had appeared almost bronzed by the glow from the fire in Ned's study that first night, arms, muscled and straining, lifting her, guiding her to the swell of manhood jutting from the tangle of dark hair between his powerfully built legs.

The groan of the springs told her when he reached the bed. The bed she'd shared with him.

She rolled onto her side, hauling the quilt over her shoulder and its hemmed edge to her mouth to stifle the sob that built. The gold wedding band he'd slipped on her finger cut into her palm.

God help her, but she yearned to be in that same bed with him.

Beyond the kitchen window, the sun dawned slowly, lightening the sky in bands of varying shades of pink, blue and lavender. The aroma of freshly baked bread filled the kitchen while heat from the ovens helped chase the early-morning chill from the room. As was her routine, while the bread finished baking, Gayla rolled dough for the piecrusts she would need to finish the diner's order. Two cherry, two apple and three apricot. Gertie Carson's order seldom varied. Nor did the time it was due to be delivered, Gayla fretted as she stole a glance at her watch. Almost seven and she'd promised Gertie she'd be there by nine.

Shoving a wisp of hair from her forehead with the back of her wrist, she quickly settled a circle of crust in each of the aluminum pans and began to crimp the edges.

In another part of the house, her husband slept. Gayla's fingers faltered momentarily and she forced herself to take a deep breath, unconsciously rubbing the ball of her thumb against the back of the wedding band that adorned her left hand.

In name only, she told herself, then repeated more firmly, *in name only.* The phrase had become a litany, repeated at least a hundred times a day since she'd first agreed to marry Brett, but none more than last night, her first night as his wife. She hadn't slept a wink all night. Taking another deep breath, she wondered how she would ever survive the next six months.

If she hadn't been so weak, she scolded herself, and vulnerable, she would never have had sex with him. Sex, she repeated firmly. That was what had transpired between them—not lovemaking, as she had so blindly assumed while in the midst of it all. Nothing but pure, unadulterated sex.

In name only, she repeated. Brett himself had laid the ground rules for their marriage and there was nothing she could do to change that.

She levered the bread from the ovens, pushed in the pies, then glanced at her watch again. If nothing delayed her, she would just make it to the diner on time. Her shoulders rose and fell on a weary sigh. But even if she was a little late she knew Gertie would understand.

Gertie. Gayla caught her lower lip between her teeth. Oh, dear. How would she ever explain to the woman who was almost like a mother to her that she'd married a man whom she'd known for less than three days?

Gertie held the door wide with her hip while she slid three boxes from beneath Gayla's chin. "Had me worried there for a while," Gertie said gruffly as Gayla maneuvered past her. "With all the gossip that's flying, I thought for sure I wouldn't have bread or dessert to serve today."

Gayla levered the boxes onto the stainless-steel counter, avoiding Gertie's gaze. "What gossip?" she asked innocently, unable to believe the news of her marriage was already out.

"That you up and married some stranger, that's what gossip!" Gertie shut the back door and locked it, then shuffled into the kitchen as fast as her stiff, arthritic legs would carry her, trailing Gayla like a hound on a scent. "Ned's grandson, they say. Christine's son." She caught Gayla by the elbow and spun her around to face her. "What I want to know is, is it true?"

Gayla lifted the lid on a box. "Is that all they're saying?" she asked uneasily.

"No, there's more, but first I want to hear it from your own lips. Is it true?"

Gayla kept her hands busy unpacking the boxes, unable to look Gertie in the eye. "Yes, it's true," she murmured.

Gertie sagged against the counter, setting the pans that hung above it to rattling. ''Well, I'll be hanged,'' she muttered on a disbelieving breath. ''Why'd you do it, girl?''

''Why does any woman get married?'' she replied, neatly avoiding answering the question.

Gertie narrowed an eye. ''So that's the way of it.'' Pursing her lips, she eyed Gayla warily. ''Well, I won't be asking again, you can be sure.'' She sniffed, obviously hurt that Gayla wouldn't confide in her. ''I guess this means you won't be doing my baking for me any longer, you having a rich husband and all, huh?''

Gayla couldn't stand to see Gertie hurt—not after all the kindnesses the woman had shown her over the years, and Gertie would never pry. She was that kind of friend, which made Gayla feel that much worse. But she'd promised Brett that she would tell no one but John Thomas the true reasons behind their marriage. He'd insisted that with them living in the house alone for the next six months, making their marriage public knowledge would spare Gayla's reputation any more harm. Gayla knew, though, that in a small town like Braesburg a marriage certificate wouldn't keep the people from talking—not with her reputation.

Before Gertie could turn away, Gayla caught her hands, wanting to reassure her friend. ''Of course, I'll continue to do your baking, Gertie. Nothing's changed.''

''Nothing?'' Gertie arched an eyebrow high on her wrinkled forehead. ''Things are always a-changing, girl, 'less you're dead.'' She sighed, letting go of her anger with Gayla. ''Have you got time for a cup of coffee?''

Gayla glanced at her watch. She knew she should return to Parker House in case Brett woke up and wanted breakfast. But she hated to disappoint Gertie. Brett would just have to wait.

She forced a bright smile. ''I do, if you do.''

Satisfied, Gertie led the way from the kitchen to the front of the diner. The breakfast crowd was thinning and only the coffee drinkers lingered. Gayla filled two cups, then headed for a booth by the front window while Gertie checked out a customer at the register. The bell over the entrance jingled as the door opened. Gayla glanced that way and stopped short when she saw Brett step inside.

Her breath caught at the unexpected sight of him. He looked so devastatingly handsome standing there in his starched jeans and boots, his jaw clean-shaven, his hair still damp from a shower. With her heart in her throat, she watched him shrug out of his jacket and hook it on the coatrack. He turned, hitching at his belt and tucking in his shirt more neatly. When his gaze met hers, he, too, froze, the tips of his fingers caught just inside the waist of his jeans. Slowly he drew them out.

''What are you doing here?''

''What are *you* doing here?''

Their words tangled, echoing each other's question. Brett pressed his lips together in irritation. Gayla blushed.

"I came to get some breakfast," he mumbled.

Gertie watched the exchange from behind the cash register, noting the high color in Gayla's cheeks and the air of impatience that Brett wore.

Suspecting there was more between the two than met the eye, she stepped from behind the counter and took the cups from Gayla's hands. She herded the two toward a booth. "And breakfast you'll get," she assured Brett. "I'll cook up my honeymooner special. Scrambled eggs smothered in salsa, and cheese. Hash-brown potatoes with grilled onions, and hot biscuits and sausage gravy." Having guided them into a booth, she slid their coffee cups in front of them, then stuck out her hand to Brett. "Hi, I'm Gertie," she said with a grin. "Welcome to Braesburg."

Six months. Not very long when looking at the total scheme of life, but an eternity when looked at from Gayla's perspective. Six months of sharing living space with a virtual stranger—her husband. She gave herself a hard shake and whisked her cloth quickly along the mantel as if she could wipe away the conflicting truths of those statements right along with the dust.

She couldn't.

Brett Sinclair was her husband—and still very much a stranger. After sharing the house with him for a week, she certainly didn't feel she knew him any better than she did after that first night he'd spent at Parker House.

Six months, she thought with a weary sigh. The

term specified in Ned's will. It sounded more like a jail sentence than a marriage. She carefully moved the crystal candlesticks back into place on the mantel, then adjusted them as yet another worry presented itself.

How would she ever be able to change Brett's mind about Parker House in just six short months?

She needed a plan, she told herself; a scheme, an angle from which to work. As she moved about the living room dusting and straightening, she mentally reviewed her options. If these were normal circumstances and Brett and Ned had shared a normal relationship, she would play on his feelings for his grandfather, for family. But Brett's relationship with Ned was anything *but* normal. Brett despised his grandfather and had never pretended anything else.

Sighing her frustration, she shifted her thoughts to a closer focus on Brett. *Is there anything about his personality, his character that I can appeal to?* she wondered in desperation.

She paused in her dusting, letting her mind sift through all the facts she knew about him, paltry though they were. He was an only child. Both his parents were deceased. He was the president of a large corporation. As far as his personality went, he was a paradox. Temperamental, yet compassionate. Cold-blooded, yet tender. Aloof, yet—

She jumped when a string of curses ricocheted down the hall.

She frowned, then wearily shook her head. The curses were Brett's, shouted from the study, and accented with a slap of his hand against Ned's wooden desk. Although Gayla knew he would despise the comparison, he was very much like his grandfather. Stubborn, bad-tempered, foulmouthed.

Ever since he'd taken over Ned's study as his temporary office more than a week ago, the noise level in the house had changed dramatically. The phone rang constantly, the doorbell chimed, interrupting her work while she either juggled calls or signed for deliveries for Brett.

Although she cleaned up after him, for the most part she managed to avoid direct contact with him. He ate his meals in silence with either the newspaper or a bevy of printouts at his hand for company. The rest of the time he stayed holed up in Ned's study, doing God only knew what.

Which brought her right back to her current perplexity: how in the world could she get Brett to develop any affection for Parker House if he spent all his time working in the study?

Her eyes widened and a smile began to grow on her face.

That's it! she cried silently. He was a businessman, and an obsessive one, obviously, judging by the time he devoted to his own company. She would simply appeal to his business sense. All she had to do was prove to him that Parker House was successful, capable of supporting itself while generating a modest income for Brett, and she knew he would keep it. No businessman in his right mind would consciously destroy a moneymaker.

Satisfied that at last she had a plan, she lifted the

silver tea service to set aside in order to dust under it. Just as the service's clawed feet cleared the polished table, a new string of curses ricocheted down the hall, followed quickly by a loud crash. Startled, Gayla juggled the tea service to keep from dropping it. Then ran toward the study, half expecting to find Brett sprawled unconscious on the floor.

Instead, she found him sitting in the chair, his chin dipped to his chest, his fingers templed to his forehead, his shoulders rising and falling in carefully controlled breaths. The phone lay on the hardwood floor, its plastic covering shattered—the second he'd broken in so many days.

Angered by his temper tantrum, she marched across the room and gathered the pieces of the phone in her hands. "You need to learn to control that temper of yours. I can't afford to keep replacing phones."

His head jerked up, his eyes narrowed at her dangerously. "I'll pay for the damn phone."

Gayla slapped the remnants on the desk. "Fine," she replied with a haughty lift of her chin. She folded her arms beneath her breasts. "I assume you're angry with whoever you were speaking with and not about the quality of Braesburg's phone service."

Brett continued to eye her, knowing that his current frustrations were a result of more than the discussion he'd been having with Sinclair's accountant. They'd been building since the night of the wedding ceremony when Gayla had refused his offer of champagne and sought the refuge and safety of her room. He wasn't sure what he'd been offering her along with the glass, but whatever hopes he might have harbored had been dashed when she had coolly turned down his invitation and gone to her room, drawing the proverbial line on their relationship.

The frustration of knowing that she slept in the same house, in the room just below his own, was slowly driving him crazy.

"You could assume that," he acknowledged noncommittally.

"Do you always scream at your employees that way?" she asked irritably, stooping to pick up wads of paper from the floor.

"Only when they refuse to listen to reason."

"Oh, and you do?" she retorted sarcastically, straightening and tossing the trash into the wastebasket.

He found he enjoyed the verbal banter with Gayla after a week of strained silence. "I like to think so," he replied.

"You can catch more flies with sugar than with lemons."

"Who said I wanted to catch flies?"

She stopped in her fussing long enough to frown at him. "You know what I mean."

He reared back in his chair. "Yes, I believe I do." He eyed her thoughtfully for a moment. "And how would you swing a board of directors to your way of thinking?"

"With facts," she answered without hesitation. "No one can argue successfully when faced with cold, hard facts."

Intrigued, Brett leaned forward, placing his forearms on the desk. ‘‘And what if they refuse to acknowledge the facts? What then?’’

‘‘Fire them. Anyone who refuses to acknowledge facts, is a detriment to the business, not an asset.’’

Brett tossed back his head and laughed. ‘‘If only it were that easy,’’ he murmured with a regretful shake of his head.

‘‘Well, you are the president, aren’t you?’’ she reminded him, irritated that he would laugh at her suggestion. ‘‘You ought to choose men who share your ideals, your goals.’’

‘‘‘Choose’ being the operative word,’’ he replied with an arch of his brow. ‘‘I didn’t choose any of them. I inherited them.’’

‘‘So, disinherit them,’’ she told him.

‘‘Unfortunately, I’m stuck with them. My father saw to that.’’

Gayla knew nothing of Brett’s family, and this peek into his life was too tempting not to take advantage of. ‘‘How?’’ she asked, sinking into the chair opposite the desk.

‘‘He made me president of Sinclair Corporation, but reserved all the power for the board. I can’t so much as change the brand of toilet paper in the employees’ lounge without their approval.’’

Gayla didn’t even try to mask her amazement. ‘‘Why would he do that?’’

‘‘A strategic move. He made me president to appease my mother. She threatened to divorce him if he didn’t.’’

Gayla shook her head, unable to accept that kind of reasoning. ''A businessman as intelligent as your father obviously was to have built a chain of department stores like Sinclair's wouldn't succumb to that kind of blackmail.''

''He not only would, he did. He was that greedy.'' Brett had never discussed his parents' relationship with anyone before, but there was something about Gayla that inspired confidences. ''If Mother divorced him,'' he explained further, ''by law she'd have received half of everything he owned. Dad would never willingly give her a part of the business. It was easier to make me president and get Mother off his back.''

''But he's dead now. Doesn't that change everything?''

''Not for me. Everything he owned, he placed in trust, allotting my mother a monthly allowance after his death. As far as the corporation was concerned, nothing changed. The board still has the power and I have the name.''

Gayla couldn't help but feel sorry for him. Trapped as he'd been between his mother and father in an emotional tug-of-war. Nobody won in a situation like that, least of all the person caught in the middle.

''I'm sorry,'' she said, unable to think of anything else to say.

There were a lot of things that Brett would accept from Gayla, but pity wasn't one of them. ''Don't be,'' he replied in a voice stripped of all emotion. ''I don't need your pity, or want it,'' he added coolly.

* * *

Gayla knew she was a softy. Ned had accused her of that too often for her not to be aware of that particular quirk in her personality. But she would have had to have a heart of stone not to be moved by what Brett had shared of his relationship with his parents.

When she'd extended her sympathies, he'd coolly refused the offer, telling her he didn't need or want her pity. A lie, Gayla knew. He needed her sympathy; he was just too stubborn and too proud to admit it.

But that was okay, she told herself, as she updated Parker House's checkbook ledger. No one on earth had been more stubborn than Brett's grandfather, Ned Parker, and she'd successfully dealt with his stubbornness for years. She would deal with Brett, too, offering sympathy and comfort when it was needed—whether he wanted it or not. Hopefully, at the same time, she would be able to convince him to keep Parker House and not give it away. The first step was showing him the financial records on the bed-and-breakfast.

She tapped the eraser end of her pencil against her cheek as she looked over the balances, satisfied with not only her work, but with Parker House Bed-and-Breakfast's progress over the past year.

She smiled smugly. There was no way Brett Sinclair would shut down a prosperous business like Parker House—not once he saw the books.

Brett sat at his desk with a ledger spread in front of him, listening as Gayla explained the bed-and-breakfast's financial condition. She stood at his side, her left hand resting on the back of his chair, while she pointed out items of interest with her right. The scent of roses drifted just beneath his nose.

He'd grown accustomed to the fragrance, even found himself seeking it out when he walked through the house, in hopes of tracing it to its source—Gayla. That she avoided him was obvious, and when she couldn't, she moved around him like he was a land mine that might go off at the slightest jostling. He bit back a grin at the thought. Not that he blamed her. He knew he could be a bit cantankerous at times. His secretary at Sinclair's corporate headquarters made a point of telling him that on a regular basis.

Nearly drunk on the scent of roses, he only half listened as Gayla reviewed the reports. Instead, he focused on the way her blouse gaped open just a fraction with each movement of her hand, allowing the slightest peek at a breast. He remembered the feel of those breasts, soft and full; the pebbled texture of her nipple, rough beneath his tongue; her taste, the sweetest nectar he'd ever sampled.

He shifted uneasily in his chair, frowning at the direction of his thoughts—and his body's response—and made himself focus on the pages of the ledger. He wouldn't allow himself to get involved with Gayla. Not again.

"Do you keep the books?" he asked, interrupting her.

Startled by the unexpected question, Gayla glanced up. "Well, yes." She glanced at the columns of numbers, sure that he had found a mistake. "Is there a problem?"

"No." He frowned at the statements, all handwritten, concise and neatly prepared. No computer-generated reports here. No reams of papers and numbers carefully manipulated and juggled to hide any discrepancies. He waved a hand toward the ledgers. "How did you learn to do this?"

"I took bookkeeping in high school. What I didn't learn there, I picked up from books I checked out at the public library."

"No college training?"

"No."

"Why not?" he asked and watched her cheeks redden.

"Lack of funds."

He could see that he was making her self-conscious, but waste was something he abhorred, especially when there was a keen mind and talent involved. "Others have done it with scholarships and federal loans," he persisted.

"I had other responsibilities," she replied vaguely.

He pursed his lips, seeing one more thing Gayla had sacrificed for Ned Parker: an education.

Gayla didn't want to discuss her education or lack of one with Brett, she wanted to talk about Parker House. She tapped a finger against the income-and-expense statement. "Parker House's profits may seem modest compared to Sinclair's, but I think if you consider our size, and our relative newness, you can see that we have experienced our own level of success."

Brett studied the columns of entries, a frown gathering between his brows.

"There's something missing," he murmured and angled the book for a better look. "There are no salaries listed."

"As I told you before, I'm the only employee."

"Well, where is your salary, then?"

"I don't draw a salary. I work in exchange for room and board."

"Surely you have needs beyond room and board. How do you pay for those?"

Gayla lifted her chin, insulted by the implications in his query. "If you think I've embezzled money from Parker House—"

"I didn't say that."

"You implied as much." She fought to remain calm. Anger wouldn't help her convince him to keep Parker House open. "The baking I do for Gertie's Diner takes care of my personal needs."

Before he could ask any other questions, she drew a file from the stack of materials she'd laid on his desk, determined to keep his attention focused on Parker House. "Because of our lack of business capital, we kept our advertising budget to a minimum, focusing on Austin, Dallas and Houston. This year we hope to advertise on a broader scale." She flipped open the file. "My plan is to join the national register for B and B's. I've also sketched an ad to run in the *Southern Living* travel guide. An editor there hinted that she might like to do a feature article on Parker House. If she does, that'll be a bonus for us that will certainly draw some attention our way."

Brett shifted in his seat, angling his body for a better

look at Gayla. Her face was set in steely determination, her eyes bright and intense as she carefully reviewed her marketing strategy. It suddenly occurred to him that not once had she referred to her plans for Parker House in the past tense. Every comment, every strategic plan was geared for the future. She hadn't offered to review Parker House's books to familiarize him with his inheritance, he suddenly realized. She was doing a sales job on him in hopes she could persuade him to keep the place open.

He caught her wrist, stopping her when she would have flipped another ledger page. Startled, she lifted her gaze to his.

"It's no good, Gayla," he warned in a low voice.

"Wh-why, I don't know what you mean," she stammered.

"I think you do," he replied dryly. "You dragged all this in here in an attempt to persuade me to keep Parker House open as a bed-and-breakfast. Nothing you say or do will change my mind. When my six months are up, Parker House goes to the city, whether you like it or not."

"But why?" she cried in dismay. "It's a profitable business. You could keep it open. And you wouldn't have to be here or do anything. I'd run it just as I always have."

"No way," he growled as he pushed to his feet. "This house has ruined enough lives. My mother's, and I suppose—if I cared—my grandfather's. I won't stand by and watch it ruin yours, too. Nothing would please me more than to see this house torn to the ground, stone by stone."

Five

Brett sat in the study, a phone pressed to his ear, his gaze locked on the computer screen filled with the past month's sales reports. Without exception, every one of the twelve Sinclair stores showed at least a ten-percent loss. That was nothing new. For the last nine months they'd been showing a loss, but they'd never hit the ten-percent mark before.

Somewhere in the house, a hammer pounded. He suspected it was Gayla's way of seeking revenge. Just because he wouldn't agree to keep Parker House in business, she seemed determined to make his life a living hell and work all but impossible.

He knew he'd been unnecessarily cruel, but he had to make her understand that Parker House was history. There was no way that he could leave it intact without feeling as if he'd dishonored his mother's wishes. He knew that if Christine Sinclair were alive to accept the estate, she would have had the house leveled. She'd hated Parker House. The years she'd spent there, by her own admission, had been the most miserable ones of her life. Hard for Brett to believe, considering the misery he'd witnessed firsthand during the years of her marriage to his father.

Trying to keep his thoughts focused on the conversation at hand, Brett flattened his palm over the ear not already covered by the phone. "I can't cut expenses any further, Marty," he yelled into the receiver. "And you damn well know it! Personnel has already been cut to the bare minimum, advertising in half. We've even removed a third of the fluorescent light tubes in the stores to cut down on the electrical bills, and we're still showing a loss." He reared back in his chair, fighting for patience. "What we need," he said more calmly, "is to focus more on sales, not expenses. The market has changed in the last few years and we haven't kept up with the trends."

The argument was an old one, repeated at least once a month to Sinclair's board of directors, but all with the same result: a brick wall of resistance. And it was his father's fault, Brett thought in frustration. If he'd only given him power to implement his ideas, he wouldn't be facing the demise of Sinclair Corporation.

The directors had all been with the company for more than twenty years, each the head of his own department.

Combined, they formed a barrier that Brett couldn't penetrate, no matter how hard he tried.

Frustrated by their grumbling, Brett decided to end the conference call. "I'll have a copy of the proposed changes in your hands within a month. I plan to use the St. Louis store as our test market. Please," he said, hoping that for once they'd honor his request, "at least consider the proposal. The future of Sinclair's depends on your combined support."

Before anyone could argue the point, Brett hung up the phone and sagged back in his chair. With one hand covering the burning sensation in his stomach, he squeezed his forehead in the span of the other.

The sound of a hammer striking metal continued, making his headache even worse. "How in hell is a man supposed to work around here?" he yelled as he pushed himself out of his chair. He stormed out of the study, determined to put an end to the irritating noise. He followed the sound up the stairs and down the hall, but stopped in front of a bedroom, whose door was ajar.

Gayla was bent over the side of the bed, beating the living daylights out of its metal frame.

"What in the hell do you think you're doing?" he roared. He snatched the hammer from her hand and she straightened, fisting her hands on her hips. Her cheeks were flushed from her efforts and wisps of hair that had escaped the knot she'd pinned on top of her head, covered her eyes. She shoved the hair aside and glared right back at him.

"I'm trying to get this frame loose from the footboard, but it's stuck."

"Why in hell are you taking the bed apart?"

"Spring-cleaning."

"It's not spring," he snapped irritably.

"I know, but it will be soon, and then we'll have guests and there's not time for deep cleaning, so I'm doing it now." She grabbed the hammer from his hand. "Now, if you'll excuse me." She bent at the waist, holding the hammer in both hands between her spread legs. Taking a deep breath, she braced herself, then swung upward, making the metal frame sing. Unfortunately, that was all it did, for it didn't budge an inch from its carved slot in the footboard.

Frustrated by her stubbornness, Brett wrenched the hammer away. "Give me that before you kill yourself." He knelt at the corner of the bed and struck the metal frame twice. It popped free and dropped to the floor with a thud.

He rose and tossed the hammer on the bed in disgust. "I don't know why you're going to all this trouble," he said impatiently. "In a couple of months this place will be nothing but a memory."

Gayla's breasts rose and fell beneath her faded sweatshirt, her anger rising with each drawn breath. She was sick to death of being reminded that Parker House's days were numbered, and sicker still of Brett's cavalier attitude toward the house that had belonged to his family for over three generations.

"That may well be," she returned, her voice tight with barely controlled anger. "But during that time there will still be bills to pay, and Parker House has always paid its own way.'' She grabbed up the hammer. ''And in order to do that, we have to have guests.'' She took a swing at the remaining leg of the metal frame still supporting the leaning footboard.

Brett caught her hand before she could swing again. She whipped her head around to glare at him and he saw the hurt he'd caused with his callous remarks. His anger melted beneath her accusing look. ''You don't have to do this,'' he said quietly.

''This is how I earn my room and board,'' she replied. ''And have for years.''

''You don't have to earn your keep anymore, Gayla. You're my wife.''

''In name only,'' she reminded him and jerked free of his grasp. She swung the hammer again and the frame broke loose, hitting the floor with a crash. Brett caught the footboard before it fell, too, and eyed her over its polished top. ''You're stubborn as a mule, Gayla Sinclair, and I'll be damned if I'll let you work yourself to death to save this old house.''

That he'd used the name she now shared with him, didn't register, she was so mad. ''And just exactly how do you plan to stop me?'' she retorted.

He eased the footboard against the wall and met her defiant gaze. He wondered if she realized how utterly desirable she looked, standing there, her cheeks flushed with anger, her breasts thrust stubbornly against the thin sweatshirt she wore. He was tempted to throw her on the bed, and make love to her until she forgot about Parker House and her misguided loyalty to it and its prior owner. But he'd done that once and still lived with the shame. So instead, he heaved a deep sigh. "I'm not," he replied. "I'm going to help."

Brett's offer to help with the spring-cleaning was a godsend, but one Gayla wasn't quite ready to acknowledge. With his assistance, came a forced closeness—something she had tried to avoid at all costs. They bumped shoulders, brushed hands, knocked heads while they worked, each encounter increasing the tension that already had her nerves stretched tighter than taffy on a pull.

She felt as if she had been ripped in two, with one part of her despising Brett for his stubborn refusal to keep Parker House open, while the other part—the part that shamed her—yearned for him. She couldn't look at him without remembering what had passed between them that first night—the compassion she'd found in his arms, the gentleness of his touch, the passion they'd shared.... But after, the humiliation when she'd discovered the next morning that he'd left without so much as a goodbye; the insult he'd added to injury when she'd found the money he'd left on his bed.

With each passing day, she grew more aware of his presence in the house, even found pleasure in the extra work his living there created for her. She did for him what a wife would do...except climb into his bed and satisfy the other needs she knew were there.

She tried not to think of these things as she worked alongside him, choosing to focus instead on the bonus his offer to help presented. Whether he realized it or not, Brett was helping to prepare Parker House for the new season in spite of his adamancy to see the house destroyed.

They moved mattresses to the balcony for airing, polished headboards and footboards, dragged the furniture away from the walls, with Gayla growing more smug in her knowledge with each accomplished task. But when she dropped to her knees at the baseboards, armed with a bucket of warm, sudsy water and an old rag, Brett balked.

"What now?" he demanded to know.

"We have to wash the baseboards," she replied, dipping the rag into the water.

"Why?"

"To wash away a year's worth of dust."

"Dammit, I've got a corporation to run," he said with growing frustration. "I don't have time to act as some scullery maid."

"I didn't ask for your help," she reminded him sweetly.

She watched the muscles in his jaw work, sure that he would leave. But he dropped down beside her and snatched the rag from her hand, putting muscle behind his movements as he rubbed furiously at the painted wood. She tried not to smile at the sight of him scrubbing baseboards on a house he swore he would see destroyed.

He glanced up at her and caught her watching him. "What?" he demanded irritably.

"Nothing," she said brightly and pulled another dripping rag from the water.

"Nothing, hell. You're laughing at me."

Gayla looked at him, her expression all innocence. "No, I'm not. I'm simply smiling. You should try it sometime."

Brett rocked back on his heels. "I smile," he blustered defensively.

"I'm sure you do," she responded reasonably as she squeezed sudsy water from the rag back into the bucket. "Just not in my presence."

Brett would have argued the point, but he couldn't think of the last time he'd smiled in her presence or out. Sobered by the thought, he watched her cheerfully scrub at the baseboard while she hummed some little ditty of a song.

"You've got soap on your nose."

Gayla straightened, rubbing furiously at the end of her nose. "I do? Where?"

He caught her hand and forced it to her side, then lifted his own to wipe away the glob of bubbles that clung to the side of her nose. She lifted her gaze to his, startled at first by the strength of his hand on hers, then transfixed by the gentleness of his touch, the heat that darkened his blue eyes. Knee-to-knee, they stared at each other over the width of his hand.

The fall was simultaneous, each unsure who had moved first. But that they were pressed chest-to-chest, their arms locked tightly around each other, their mouths hungrily seeking, neither could deny. The tension Gayla had found in his presence slowly slipped away, leaving her boneless and helpless against the assault of emotions that ripped through her.

She was scared to death that she was falling in love with this man, and yet she couldn't deny that she needed him, yearned for him daily with the urgency of a woman long denied. Emotions shifted, giving way to sensations she was only just beginning to understand. Then, without warning, he pushed away.

"I'm sorry," he gasped, holding her at arm's length, his breathing ragged. "I shouldn't have done that."

Gayla gathered her fingers around the rag she still held, fisting it into a tight ball, her gaze locked on his. "It takes two, Brett," she replied stiffly, then turned her attention on the baseboard and began scrubbing with a vengeance.

Surprised that she would demand part of the blame instead of laying it all on him, Brett could only stare. He'd taken advantage of her once, would have again just moments ago, if he hadn't come to his senses in time. But instead of being angry with him for the slip, she seemed more angry that he'd stopped.

Slowly he pushed to his feet. He had to get away from her, he told himself, before he was tempted to finish what he'd started—something he knew they would both live to regret.

Brett sat at the round table in the garden room with Gayla on his right and John Thomas at his left. He was irritated that Gayla had invited his grandfather's attorney for dinner without first discussing it with him. Why, he wasn't sure.

He supposed it could be the fact that the man's face lit up with a smile every time he looked at Gayla, but curved into a frown each time he glanced Brett's way. Or perhaps it was the fact that the two carried on a running conversation, totally ignoring him, their heads tipped together, gossiping about people around town like two old ladies with nothing better to do.

Dammit, as much as he hated to admit it, he was jealous. He didn't like the attention John was paying Gayla, nor the way she smiled and laughed with him in return. He wanted her to smile that way at him, those brown eyes of hers twinkling with laughter. And he wanted her to touch him the way she kept touching John. Light, flirtatious touches of her fingertips on his sleeve or on the back of his hand, while she talked.

Inwardly, he groaned. What was the matter with him? Was he that starved for female attention that he would begrudge an old geezer like John Thomas a few minutes of harmless flirting with a beautiful young woman? Granted, he'd been feeling a little like a caged lion lately—sharing the house with Gayla, but not her bed. And that was the problem, he finally admitted. He wanted to share her bed.

But no one knew better than Brett what a mistake that would be. In less than four months he would be leaving Braesburg...and Gayla. Getting physically involved with her would only make leaving her that much more difficult. He was already beginning to realize how much he would miss her when he returned to Kansas City.

"Are we going to have dessert, or not?" he gruffed impatiently.

Both Gayla's and John's heads turned as if drawn by a single string. They stared at him in openmouthed surprise. Gayla was the first to speak. "Of course we are," she murmured and quickly gathered the empty dinner plates. After placing them on the buffet, she returned with dessert plates.

"Carrot cake." John sighed and gave his stomach a delighted pat. "I always have room for some of your carrot cake, Gayla."

If she'd served him a plate of congealed cod-liver oil, Brett suspected John's response would have been the same.

John cut a generous bite with his fork, then frowned at Brett. "How long you been here now, Brett? About a month?"

"Closer to two," Brett replied. He knew because he religiously crossed off each day on the calendar of his planner.

John nodded toward the dessert plate Gayla had set in front of Brett. "Aren't you going to eat your dessert?"

Brett shoved the plate away. "I believe I've had a stomachful, thank you," he muttered.

John's frown deepened. "I see you inherited your mother's temperament."

"Among other things," Brett replied dryly.

The first smile John had directed his way slowly

chipped at the corner of his mouth. "Yep, you're Christine's son, no doubt about that." He laughed fully, dragging his napkin from his knee to dab at the corners of his mouth. "She was a sour little thing, always whining and complaining."

To have her described in such a derogatory manner didn't bother Brett. No one knew better than he how unpleasant his mother could be. But he was surprised to learn that she'd been that way as a child, as well. Oh, he'd known how she'd hated her father, but he'd always thought her dissatisfaction with life stemmed more from her marriage to *his* father than from anything that had transpired before.

"You knew her?" he asked, unable to contain his curiosity.

"Everybody in town knew Christine. Ned dragged her everywhere he went. Mostly because he couldn't find anyone brave enough to keep her after Mrs. Parker passed on. She was a pill, that one. Throwing temper tantrums, threatening to kill herself if she didn't get her way." He wagged his head, unaware of the sudden tension that tightened Brett's face. "I don't how Ned put up with all the shenanigans she pulled." He lifted his head and looked at Brett. "How old was she when she died, anyway?"

"Fifty-four."

"Young, still," John murmured with a regretful shake of his head. "Was she ill for long?"

"No," Brett mumbled, wishing now that he hadn't pursued the subject of his mother. "She wasn't ill at all."

John looked at him in puzzlement. "How did she die, then?"

"Suicide."

Brett heard the tiny gasp that escaped Gayla's lips but refused to look her way. He knew he would find pity in her eyes and he didn't want it.

John fell back against the back of his chair. "Suicide!" he exclaimed. "Dear God. As often as she threatened, I never believed she'd really kill herself. Considered it childish hysterics she'd grow out of someday." He sat for a moment in silence, his forehead plowed in a thoughtful frown. "How'd she do it?" he finally asked.

"Carbon-monoxide poisoning. I found her in her car in the garage, the engine running, the garage doors closed."

John's eyes softened and he leaned to clasp a hand around Brett's shoulder and squeezed. "I'm sorry, son. That must have been tough."

Unaccustomed to physical displays of emotion from a man, Brett tensed beneath John's hand at the sympathetic gesture. Yes, it had been tough, he remembered, but he'd been prepared for the scene long before his mother had actually succeeded in ending her life. He'd always considered her suicide attempts as a cry for attention, but this time he hadn't arrived soon enough to give her what she craved.

"Why did she do it? Was she depressed?" John asked.

"No, not really. Just angry. When my father died, he left his estate in a trust with strict instructions on the monthly allotment that was to be given to my mother.''

''And it wasn't enough to meet living expenses?''

''For most people, but not my mother.''

John nodded knowingly, more than aware of Christine's extravagant ways. ''She should have come home to Parker House. Ned would have welcomed her back.''

Welcomed her back? Brett doubted it, especially since the old man was the one who'd kicked her out in the first place. But what good would it do to argue the point now? Ned and Christine were both dead. Nothing could change that.

Brett shot out of his chair, the phone pressed to his ear.

''What do you mean, you won't consider my proposal?'' he roared into the phone receiver, the blood boiling in his veins.

''I didn't say we *wouldn't* consider your proposal, Brett,'' Marty, Sinclair's accountant and spokesperson for the board of directors, explained in an obvious attempt to calm Brett. ''Only that we won't consider it until this six-month stint of yours is up and you're back in Kansas City.''

Brett slapped the flat of his hand against the desktop, sending pens rolling and paper flying. ''Dammit! Sinclair's won't be around in six months if we don't act immediately!''

''Now, now, Brett,'' Marty soothed reasonably. ''You're not talking rationally. And it's no wonder, what with all the pressure you're currently living under. The stress of settling your grandfather's estate, your grief over his passing. And all coming right on the heels of your mother's death."

Brett could hear his blood pounding in his ears, the sound like a symphony of kettledrums.

"The decision's made, Brett," Marty said. "The board met and voted to delay the discussion on your proposal until your return to Kansas City in August."

Brett's roar of anger and the crash that followed echoed throughout the house. Gayla heard it from as far away as the kitchen. Sure that something dire had occurred, she shoved the milk carton back into the refrigerator and took off down the hall. By the time she reached the study, the phone was lying on the floor where Brett had thrown it and Brett himself was sitting behind the desk staring at the opposite wall, his eyes glazed. Something about his look warned her that this was not one of his typical temper tantrums.

Quietly she crossed to the desk. "Brett, what's happened?"

He lifted his gaze to stare at her, his eyes dull and lifeless. "They won't consider the proposal that I sent for the changes to Sinclair's until I return to Kansas City in August."

Fully aware of the hours Brett had spent preparing the proposal, Gayla understood his anger. "But why?" she asked, her forehead creased in puzzlement.

"They don't have a reason, nor do they need one. The board can do anything they damn well please."

"Oh, Brett, I'm—"

His hand shot up like a traffic cop's, nearly clipping off the end of her nose. "If you say you're sorry, I swear I'll throw this computer monitor through the wall," he warned, laying a hand on the monitor that sat on the edge of his desk.

Gayla bit back a smile.

She stooped to pick up the phone from the floor where Brett had thrown it. Surprisingly, it was still intact. "Well, since I hate to see perfectly good equipment destroyed, I'll keep my sympathies to myself." She set the phone on the desk, gently replacing the receiver in its cradle, the smile still chipping at the corner of her mouth.

"I'm sure glad you think this is funny," Brett said, scowling at her. "I worked my ass off for over a month getting that damn proposal ready and now they won't even look at it."

"I wasn't laughing at the situation," she said pointedly. "I was laughing at you."

"I'm thrilled you find me so entertaining," he replied dryly.

She laughed then, fully. "It's not you, really. It's your temper."

That comment won a frown.

Gayla chuckled. "If you could only see yourself, you'd laugh, too. You're like a giant-size two-year-old who throws a fit when he doesn't get his way."

"It's not a matter of my getting my way," he said in disgust. "My concerns are for the corporation.

Without some immediate changes, Sinclair's stands to fall into bankruptcy.''

Gayla's smile melted away. She hadn't been aware how serious Sinclair's financial problems were. ''Isn't there anything you can do to change their minds?''

''Nothing.''

''You're sure?''

''Absolutely. With me stuck down here in Braesburg, they've got me over a barrel.''

''I'm sor—'' At Brett's warning glance, she cut short her offer of sympathy. Narrowing her eyes, she squared her shoulders, and frowned at him. ''Well, I am sorry,'' she said in open defiance of his wishes, ''whether you're willing to accept my sympathy or not.'' With a toss of her head, she turned her back on him and strode angrily from the office.

''Gayla!'' Brett roared. ''Gayla! Where are you?''

Gayla dumped a load of clean towels at the foot of the stairs and heaved a sigh as she headed for the study. She'd thought with the pressures of preparing the proposal behind him, that Brett's bad moods and fits of temper would diminish. They hadn't. He'd just shifted his attention to dissolving Ned's estate, which seemed to have the same effect on him as had dealing with Sinclair's financial problems.

''I'm right here,'' she answered calmly as she stepped into the study. ''What's wrong now?''

Brett slapped the back of his hand against the paper he held. ''Who are all these people?'' he demanded to know.

Unsure who or what he was referring to, Gayla moved behind the desk to look at the piece of paper he held. "They're all friends of Ned's," she replied, scanning the list of outstanding debts. "Friends he loaned money to over the years."

"Hell, what was the old man—a retailer or a banker?"

Gayla bit back a smile. "A little of both, probably, but mostly a friend."

Brett dropped his forehead to the flat of his hand, groaning. "Do you realize that the only real asset on this list, other than Parker House, is the commercial property downtown?"

Before she could answer, he shoved back the chair, making Gayla jump to keep from being mowed over. "Where did he keep his keys?"

"The keys to the hardware store?" she asked in confusion.

"Yes, the keys to the hardware store," he replied, mocking her. "That is what we're talking about, isn't it?"

Accustomed to his coarse behavior and unaffected by it, Gayla opened the bottom drawer and pulled out a worn cigar box. She lifted the lid and poked through an assortment of keys until she found the one she wanted. She held it out to Brett.

"The electricity is still on, so lighting shouldn't be a problem. But I feel I should warn you," she added. "No one has been inside the store since Ned closed the doors eight years ago. It's probably a mess."

"What isn't, around here?" he retorted dryly, and took the key from her palm.

Gayla's warning had been mild, considering the actual condition of the old store. When Brett shouldered open the door, a mélange of scents overwhelmed him, the worst of which was a result of the rat droppings littering the floor.

"Jesus," he muttered, waving the air beneath his nose. He groped along the wall until he found the panel of switches and flipped them on. Most of the overhead bulbs remained dark, but a few of the fluorescent tubes blinked on. He wandered in, stepping carefully, jumping occasionally when he heard a scurrying sound behind him. Peg-board stretched from ceiling to floor on his right and held an assortment of equipment. A mesh of spider webs covered round bins heaped high with nails and screws.

He put a toe to a sack of cement on a low shelf and the paper dissolved at his touch, sending clouds of cement dust to thicken the air. With a weary shake of his head, he walked on.

At the back of the store, a squared-off space was surrounded by a half wall of glass. A rusted metal sign nailed to the wooden door simply read Office. He tried the knob and found it unlocked. He pushed open the door, his skin crawling as the hinges gave with a spine-shivering screech. He hit the switch by the door and a single light bulb swinging from the ceiling popped on.

Like the rest of the store, the office held a damp,

musty odor. A scarred wooden desk dominated most of the space, and behind it loomed a huge black safe. A beat-up sofa sat beneath the half wall of glass, its tattered cushions an obvious nest for the mice and other critters who now called the place home.

"Brett?"

He wheeled guiltily at the sound of Gayla's voice. "Back here!" he yelled and quickly flipped off the light and closed the office door.

They met in the middle of the paint aisle, surrounded by stacks of gallon-size metal buckets with faded labels. "What are you doing here?" he asked irritably.

She shrugged, hugging her jacket closer to her chest. "I figured turnabout is fair play. You helped me with my spring-cleaning, I'll help you with yours."

Brett frowned. "I'm not spring-cleaning. I just need to go through all this junk to see if there is anything of value. I really don't need or expect you to help."

"No," she agreed with a nod. "But I'm here anyway. So, where do we start?" she asked, looking around.

"Got a match?"

Gayla twisted her head around to stare at him, then laughed when she saw the look of disgust on his face.

Feeling generous, she gave him a pat on the back as she walked past him. "It's not as bad as it looks," she replied cheerfully. "A good cleaning, and it will look a lot better."

Six

Hours later, Gayla stood before the line of gunmetal-gray file cabinets, her jeans covered in dust and her sweatshirt sleeves pushed to her elbows. She sifted through the old file drawers, methodically throwing away a half century's accumulation of worthless paper.

She'd already made two trips to the Dumpsters in the alley behind the store and it appeared, she thought with a glance at the wastebasket, she would make several more before she was through. Deciding she needed—and deserved—a break, she went in search of Brett.

She found him standing on the sidewalk in front of the store, his arms folded across his chest, staring intently down the street. He struck an impressive pose—

tall, brooding, the wind playing havoc with his dark hair. She stopped and simply stared, allowing herself the pleasure of studying him unobserved.

He was a handsome man with strong features, carved by the ancestors he damned on a daily basis. That he had hated his grandfather was no secret, but Gayla couldn't help wondering if his feelings would have been the same if he'd actually known Ned.

She'd loved Ned, and if she wasn't careful, she knew she would fall in love with his grandson, as well. She didn't mind admitting—if only to herself—that she was attracted to him. Which was surprising, since he did nothing but frown and growl at her daily. Yet, a night didn't pass that she didn't long to climb those stairs and crawl into his bed just to experience the passion again.

Shaking off the unsettling thoughts, she stepped outside. "What are you doing?"

Without looking at her, Brett nodded toward the steady stream of traffic easing down Main Street. "Where are all those cars going?"

Gayla followed the direction of his gaze. "To the sausage factory, I'd imagine," she replied with a shrug.

"A sausage factory?" he repeated, twisting his head around to frown at her.

"Not a factory, really, not like you'd imagine. It's a small place, run by the Hilliards. The business has been in their family for years."

Brett turned once again to stare down the street. "Is it like this all the time?" he asked curiously.

"The traffic?" she asked. At his nod, she replied, "Yes, I guess so, though I really never thought about it before."

Brett waved at the vacant stores scattered up and down the street. "Why are all these places closed?"

"Lack of business. One of those super chain stores opened on the edge of town several years ago." She gave a shrug. "The smaller stores couldn't compete with their chain-store prices."

"Fools," he mumbled, as if to himself.

"Excuse me?" Gayla responded, unsure whom he was calling a fool.

"Fools," he repeated and caught her by the hand. "Let's take a walk."

The intimate grasp of his hand on hers was unexpected. He walked quickly, forcing Gayla to almost run to match his long stride. He stopped at the first empty store. "What was here?"

"A pharmacy. They went out of business about three years after Ned closed the hardware store."

Brett dropped her hand, curling his into a fist to swipe at the dirty front window. "Is that a soda fountain?" he asked, pressing his nose against the glass for a better look.

"Yes, Mr. Morley's wife ran it. She made the best malts and shakes in the state."

Again he caught her hand in his and strode on, dragging Gayla behind him. He stopped at the next vacant storefront. A crude sign—For Sale or Lease—was taped inside the window. "What about this place? What was it?"

"A grocery store."

Brett backed up to the curb, lifting his gaze, studying the building, his mouth puckering in a thoughtful frown.

Without a word, he whirled and bolted across the street, dodging the occasional car. Gayla followed. "What on earth are you doing?" she asked breathlessly when she reached his side.

Brett waved a hand at the storefronts opposite him. "Look at that," he said in disgust. "In an effort to modernize their stores and compete with the chain store, they slapped up all that metal siding, covering up the original brick fronts."

Surprised by the emotion filling his voice, Gayla followed his gaze. "So?"

"They should have saved themselves the money and played on the old rather than trying to compete with the larger chain. They should have changed their marketing strategy, focused on what they did best. They should have catered to a different level of consumer, providing hard-to-find staples, gourmet items, custom cuts of meat. If they had, they'd still be in business."

He shifted slightly, waving a hand at the pharmacy. "Take the drugstore, there. Granted, they might not be able to compete on the same level price-wise, but they should have focused on their strengths, not their weaknesses. They should have offered home delivery, specialized their services to meet the needs of their customers. Maybe even expanded their inventory to include gift items." He whirled to face her, his eyes burning bright with an enthusiasm Gayla had never seen before. ''How many soda fountains are in this town?''

''None.''

''Exactly,'' he replied, as if he'd known her answer before she'd voiced it. ''And where are all these people coming from who visit the sausage factory?''

''All over the state.''

''And after a long trip, you know they must be hungry or thirsty. They'd see the sign for the soda fountain, be charmed by the quaintness of the place, come in for a cold drink and a snack and wind up leaving with a purchase or two tucked under their arm.''

Gayla began to understand. She turned to look at the vacant buildings, seeing them in a new light. ''It's a shame no one thought of that,'' she murmured.

''Not a shame, a waste,'' he muttered in disgust and strode back across the street, his hands stuffed deep into the pockets of his jeans.

Gayla stood for a moment, staring, then ran after him. She caught up with him at the door to the hardware store. ''If you think it's a waste, why don't you do something about it?'' she challenged.

''Like what?'' he growled impatiently.

''Like organize all the owners of the buildings, share your ideas with them. I'll bet you could even think of a use for this old store,'' she said with an expansive wave of her hand. ''Maybe you could turn it into an old general store or perhaps a shop for local crafts.''

Brett's eyes narrowed dangerously. ''No way,

lady,'' he warned, stubbornly folding his arms across his chest. ''I didn't come here to save the town. I came to close an estate. I'm selling this place to the first available buyer. And if no one makes an offer, when my six months are up, the city gets it, lock, stock, and barrel.''

''But, Brett—''

He cut her off with an impatient wave of his hand. ''Six months. That's it.''

Frustrated, Gayla glared at his back as he walked away. ''And you thought Ned was stingy and mean,'' she muttered under her breath.

He wheeled around, his eyes blazing, obviously having heard her. ''And what's that supposed to mean?''

''Exactly what it implies,'' she said angrily. ''Here you have all this expertise that would help these people restore their businesses, but you're too darn selfish to share it. Oh, forget it,'' she said when she saw the stubborn set of his jaw. ''I'm going home.''

Brett worked until his back ached from the unaccustomed strain, his anger at Gayla feeding his need for physical release. She'd taken his own suggestions and thrown them in his face in an attempt to suck him into staying. Behind it all was her desire to save Parker House, he was sure.

Flattening his hands on the small of his back, he arched in an attempt to get out the kinks. He wasn't staying, he told himself. And nothing that Gayla Matthews Sinclair did or said would change his mind.

Weary, he headed for the rear of the store and Ned's office. He flipped on the overhead light, then he sat, uncomfortable in this chair he knew had once been his grandfather's, and looked around the room. A calendar was nailed to one wall, its date eight years old almost to the month. With a sigh, he turned his attention to the filthy desk.

He dug his handkerchief from his pocket and swiped several years' worth of dust from the desk's glass top. With the removal of the dust, he discovered several pictures lay beneath the streaked glass. Finding a letter opener in the drawer, he lifted the corner of the glass and eased out the photographs. They were faded with age and brittle to the touch. Shuffling them into a neat stack, he studied the face on the first and assumed it must be his grandmother, taken before her marriage to Ned, judging by her youthful look. The next photo was a studio print of a man and woman posed with a young girl sitting in the woman's lap.

He frowned at the print, knowing that he was looking at a picture of Ned Parker's family. The old man—not so old in the photo—stood behind his wife and daughter, looking dapper in a double-breasted, pinstriped suit, his chest swelled in pride. The woman had a fragile look about her, but wore a loving smile as she rested a hand on the shoulder of a sulky-faced child.

His mother. He angled the picture for more light. Although the picture was black-and-white and years old, he recognized her. The shape of the eyes, the nose, the pouty curve of her lips. He remembered that expression—it was the one she wore most often. Feeling guilty for the disloyal thought, he tossed aside the pictures and started yanking open drawers.

Yellowed invoices, bent paper clips, wooden paint stirrers bearing the logo of Parker's Hardware. He sifted through the worthless accumulation until he uncovered a packet wrapped in brown paper and tied with a piece of twine. Retrieving it from the drawer, he reared back in the chair and pulled the knot free, thinking that maybe he'd found something of value.

The wrapping paper crackled, then slipped away, revealing a handful of envelopes, each addressed to Christine Parker, 121 Summit, Kansas City, Missouri. The address wasn't familiar to Brett, but the name certainly was. The return address was Ned Parker, No. 1 Oak Knoll, Braesburg, Texas. Penned across the length of the envelope were the words "Return to Sender, Addressee Unknown." Brett frowned, recognizing his mother's own unique handwriting; the sweeping leg of the *R*, the delicate scrolling of the *S*. He turned the envelope over and saw that the seal had never been broken.

But she'd said her father had never contacted her, his mind argued defensively. There must be some mistake. He broke the seal on one envelope and carefully unfolded the page.

His heart grew heavier and heavier in his chest as he read the impassioned pleas of Ned Parker, begging his only child to come home.

Gayla looked at the clock again, and caught her lower lip between her teeth. "What in the world is keeping him?'' she worried out loud. She'd been home for hours. Cooked dinner, eaten and put a plate for Brett in the oven, and still he hadn't returned.

Surely he isn't still at the store working? she told herself. Not this late. But where else would he have gone? She walked to the kitchen window, hugging her arms beneath her breasts, feeling guilty for having argued with him.

The building was more than likely unsafe after being empty for so many years. Fearing that he'd hurt himself in some way, she quickly headed out the door.

She found his truck parked in front of the hardware store and the door to the building unlocked. She opened the front door. The lights were still on, but she didn't see a sign of Brett anywhere.

''Brett?'' she called uncertainly. ''Brett? Are you here?'' She stepped inside and pulled the door closed behind her, listening.

She cautiously walked down the littered aisles, looking left and right. ''Brett?'' she called again. She noticed the light coming from Ned's old office and quickly turned down the aisle that led to it. Brett sat before Ned's desk, with his forearms draped along the chair's arms, his hands dangling limply just above his knees. His eyes were open and staring, but he remained motionless, oblivious to her presence.

''Brett? Are you okay?'' she asked as she eased inside.

He didn't answer but continued to stare trance-like at the papers strewn across the desk.

His stillness frightened her. She picked up a letter from the desk, but before she had a chance to read it, Brett's voice stopped her.

"She lied," he said in a low voice. "She lied about everything."

Gayla glanced up at him and saw that his gaze was still fixed on the desktop. "Who lied?" she prodded gently.

"Mother. She said he'd kicked her out and told her never to come back. She said that never once in all those years had he ever contacted her." Suddenly he lunged forward, swiping the letters to the floor in one furious stroke. "Lies," he repeated. "All lies."

His anger frightened her more than his stillness had, moments ago. "Let's go home, Brett," she said, anxious to get him away from whatever had upset him.

"I don't have a home. Never did."

"Sure, you do," she reminded him gently. "In Kansas City."

"No," he argued. "A house, but never a home. Mother saw to that."

Taken aback, Gayla could only stare.

"They fought all the time. Screamed accusations and obscenities at each other constantly, each blaming the other for their unhappiness. But I was the source of their unhappiness and neither of them had the nerve to send me away."

"You're just upset," Gayla soothed, taking his hand and tugging him to his feet, determined to get him away from whatever nightmares he'd uncovered.

"She made him leave," he murmured, as if she

hadn't spoken. "Chased him away with her constant demands and complaining. She'd gotten pregnant with me on purpose so he'd have to marry her. He told me that before he died." He turned to look at Gayla, his eyes now void of any emotion. "He hated me for that," he said dully. "Almost as much as he hated her."

Gayla couldn't listen to any more. He was breaking her heart. She grabbed his jacket from the chair and threw it over his shoulders, guiding him quickly from the office. Once outside, she didn't give him a chance to argue, but led him straight to her car.

They made the return trip to Parker House in silence with Brett slumped despondently in the seat beside her. Once home, she led him up the stairs and to his room. She stripped the jacket from his shoulders, and with a gentle nudge to his chest, he sank onto the bed.

"You need to rest," she told him firmly. "Everything will look differently in the morning."

She started to leave, but stopped when she realized he hadn't moved but continued to sit where she'd left him. She'd grown accustomed to his gruffness and his blistering fits of temper, and much preferred that to this quiet despondency.

Unable to leave him in this depressed state, she went back to him and stooped to pull off his boots, then hesitated only slightly before working the buttons free from his shirt. When he still didn't move to help her, she drew a shuddery breath and peeled the shirt from his shoulders and down his arms, baring his chest. The sight of his chest brought memories singing back, weakening her knees and her resolve to remain unaffected by him. She wanted desperately to curl up against that wall of strength and lay her cheek over the warmth of his heart.

Stop it! she chided silently and forced her hands to his waist. Her fingers shook uncontrollably as she fumbled his belt loose, then worked his jeans over his hips and down his legs.

She yanked back the bedspread and guided him beneath the sheets. Having done all she could to make him comfortable, she switched off the bedside lamp and turned to leave. His hand caught hers at the wrist, stopping her. "Don't leave," he begged in a low voice. "Please, don't leave."

The desperation in his voice made her turn. He loosened his grip, letting his hand slide until his fingers closed around hers, his gaze locked on hers. "Please?"

Gayla sank to the edge of the bed, tightening her own fingers around his. "I won't leave you," she promised.

With a moan, he hauled her against his chest. She felt the shudder of muscle against her cheek as at last the emotions he'd held in so fiercely broke free. Tipping her face to his, she saw that tears wet his cheeks. She wound her arms around his neck and drew his face to her breasts. She soothed him, much as he had her when she'd grieved over the loss of Ned, rocking him slowly in her arms, holding him close until the storm had passed.

"I'm sorry," he murmured, drawing away, obviously embarrassed by his emotional display.

He lifted his hand, intending to swipe the remaining tears from his eyes, but Gayla replaced his hand with her lips. She tenderly pressed them to his eyes, to his cheeks, kissing away the remnants of his grief. With a muffled groan, he clutched her hands in his, drawing them to his cheeks as he pressed his forehead to hers.

"I don't deserve your kindness," he mumbled miserably.

His admission touched her heart. "And why not? You certainly offered me comfort when I needed it."

He lifted his face, his gaze meeting hers. "I took advantage of you," he said, and she could see that that was truly what he thought.

"No," she countered with a vehement shake of her head. "You took nothing from me. You offered comfort, the rest just—just happened," she finished weakly, unable even now to explain what had happened between them.

The pressure of his hand tightened on hers. "It could happen again," he said, the truth of it darkening his eyes. "I wanted you then, Gayla, needed you...but not nearly as much as I do now."

Her breath caught in her throat. "I want you, too," she whispered.

"You'll stay, then?" he asked. "You'll sleep with me in my bed?"

She nodded her head. "Yes."

"And in the morning when I wake up, I won't find myself alone?"

A ghost of a smile fluttered at the corners of her mouth. ''No, I'll be here in the morning.''

He crushed her to him, then whipped back the covers and dragged her beneath them before whisking them back over them both. His lips found hers in the darkness, his fingers the tiny buttons that lined her spine. He released her long enough to drag the dress over her head, then closed his mouth over hers again, taking what she offered and giving her the passion she'd yearned for in return.

Gayla awakened slowly, the sun's bright rays nudging her from sleep. She stretched contentedly, hooking a toe in the bedcovers and dragging them down, a smile building on her lips. She froze when she caught a glimpse of Brett at her side, his head propped on his open palm, watching her.

''Good morning,'' she murmured self-consciously and pulled the sheet more modestly over her nakedness.

''We'll have none of that,'' he ordered, his voice still husky from sleep. He adjusted the sheet to where it had lain before, allowing a more open view of her breasts. Satisfied, he slung his arm around her waist and hauled her to him. ''That's better,'' he murmured as he laid his head next to hers on the pillow they'd shared through the night. ''Did you sleep well?''

''Yes,'' she whispered, her gaze locked on his, wondering how he could act as if they awoke every morning in just this way. He seemed so relaxed, while she felt as if every nerve in her body were tied up in a knot. "Did you?"

"Like a baby."

The lazy movements of his hand on her bare back acted like a balm on her nervousness. Timidly she lifted her finger to the mat of hair on his chest. His purr of contentment was all she needed to hear. She sighed and snuggled closer, deciding she liked this morning pillow-talk.

"Thank you for..." He paused, unsure how to voice his gratitude. "For...well, for staying with me," he finished in a rush.

Gayla smiled at his discomfort. "You're welcome."

"I'm sorry I yelled at you yesterday."

"Which time?"

He winced, then smoothed a wisp of hair from her cheek. "Am I that bad?"

"Worse. But don't worry, I'm used to it. Ned was grumpy, too."

Not sure that he liked the comparison, Brett frowned. "You really cared for him, didn't you?"

"Yes. He was like a father to me."

Brett rolled onto his back and slung an arm across his eyes.

Gayla rose up on an elbow to look at him. "I'm sorry. I didn't mean to upset you."

Brett lifted the arm from his eyes high enough to peer at her. Her eyes were guileless, filled with genuine concern. So unlike his mother's when she'd accused him of being just like his grandfather.

"No," he replied, then pulled her to his chest. "You didn't upset me. I'm just confused, is all."

"By what?"

"Ned Parker." His chest rose and fell in a frustrated sigh beneath Gayla's cheek. "It seems like he's almost two different people. One Mother knew, and the one you knew."

Gayla knew nothing of Ned's relationship with his daughter, but she had nothing but pleasant memories of her own relationship with him. "He was a good man, Brett. Ornery at times, stubborn at others, but basically fair in his dealings with people."

His arm tightened around her and he dipped his head to place a kiss on the top of her head. "You're an angel, Gayla. It's no wonder Ned loved you so much."

A tiny flame leaped to life in Gayla's heart at his words. She curled her fingers against his chest and shifted—wanting, needing to be closer. Inadvertently, her thigh brushed his manhood. She felt the almost instantaneous stirring, the swell of heat and strength that surged until his member prodded against the curve of her thigh. An answering heat flamed low in her abdomen and she balled her hand against his chest to keep from reaching down and touching him.

Brett felt the tension thrum through her, sensed the restraint in her clenched fist and recognized the uncertainty and need in her eyes. He smiled tenderly at her.

"Do you want to touch me?" he asked softly.

Her cheeks flamed but her chin dipped in a brief

and embarrassed nod. When she continued to hesitate, Brett caught her hand and guided it down, keeping his gaze locked on hers. At the first feather-light touch of her fingers against his sensitized flesh, he jerked, startling Gayla. Frightened that she had in some way hurt him, she tried to withdraw.

"It's okay, you didn't hurt me," he assured her, then guided her back to him, shaping her fingers around his swollen staff. Her gaze remained riveted on his as she timidly began to stroke. Growing braver, she shook free of his grasp, letting passion guide her movements. Unconsciously her hips moved, mimicking the strokes of her hand on him in a sensual grind against his leg.

With a low, satisfied moan, he gave himself up to her gentle caresses, closing his eyes against the fevered waves of pleasure that rippled through him. Up and down, tiny teasing circles, gentle flicks of a nail against the sensitive tip. Her touch was that of a sorcerer, blinding him with pleasure and stealing his mind. When he felt the last threads of sanity slipping, giving way to madness, he caught her hand in his, stilling her erotic caresses. He opened his eyes, the heat in them scorching color into Gayla's cheeks. "It's your turn," he murmured, his voice husky with promise.

He rolled her onto her back, followed her, digging his fingers into her golden hair while he nipped at first her lips, then her neck, tiny little bites that brought a delicious mix of pleasure and pain. He paused at her breasts long enough to lave each nipple into a throbbing bud, then moved on. Gayla arched against the teasing of his tongue, wanting him to linger and suckle, wanting him to end this sweet torture. But he ignored her whimpers in his downward assault on her flesh.

His tongue stroked, his teeth nipped, his lips soothed, while his clever fingers sought her petaled opening. At his touch, she gasped, shrinking away from him; but he followed, murmuring sweet promises, stroking, soothing and teasing until she allowed him entry within the warm velvet moistness. With each swirl of his finger, passion rose within her, her chest rising and falling in increasingly rapid breaths, her hands frantically clawing at the crisp sheets.

The madness returned to suck at him while he watched her, bringing him closer and closer to the edge. Kicking the bedclothing clear, he straddled her, kneeling as he guided her legs around his waist. He sank his fingers into her hips and thrust deep inside her, drawing her to him again and again, burying himself deeper and deeper within the velvety folds until he felt the first orgasmic shudder rack through her. With a strangled cry, he threw back his head and slammed her hard against him, sending them both into a wild dive over the edge of sanity.

As he tumbled through the fog, he grabbed for her, pulling her up tight against his chest.

"My angel, my sweet angel," he murmured hoarsely against her hair as the world continued to spin crazily around them.

* * *

My angel, my sweet angel...

Gayla hugged the cherished words close to her heart after she dropped Brett off at the hardware store to pick up his truck. She couldn't remember ever being called anything that pleased her more. Thoughts of him and their early-morning lovemaking kept the barest hint of a smile tugging at the corners of her mouth as she drove on to the diner to drop off the pies she'd baked that morning.

Gertie met Gayla at the diner's back door. Holding the door open with a well-padded hip, she took the top two boxes that Gayla balanced beneath her chin.

''You're late,'' she fussed good-naturedly.

Gayla staggered into the kitchen, burdened by her load. She levered the boxes onto the stainless-steel countertop, then collapsed against its edge with a weary sigh. ''I'm sorry, Gertie,'' she said. ''I overslept.''

Gertie lifted an eyebrow. ''Overslept? You?'' She made a tsking sound with her tongue. ''That new husband of yours wouldn't have anything to do with you sleeping in, now, would he?'' She laughed when Gayla's cheeks reddened. ''Girl, I'd have thought the two of you would have worn out that bed by now!''

If possible, Gayla's cheeks flamed even higher. Seeing how she'd embarrassed the younger woman, Gertie tucked her arm through Gayla's and headed toward the front. ''Nothing wrong with a healthy libido,'' she lectured. ''Why, Mr. Carson and I kept the springs humming on our bed till the day he died. God rest his soul,'' she added reverently.

Unexpected tears sprang to Gayla's eyes. The Carsons had shared a long and happy marriage—something that she knew she would never know with Brett. Six months. That was how long their marriage would last, and less than three months of that time remained. No, she and Brett certainly wouldn't be keeping any bedsprings humming.

Fresh tears welled and she waved a hand at the look of concern on Gertie's face. Emotion lodged in her throat, making any kind of explanation impossible.

Frowning, Gertie turned Gayla loose long enough to pour them each a cup of coffee. Herding Gayla ahead of her, she juggled the cups as she headed for a booth beneath the front window.

Easing her generous body into the booth, she shoved a cup towards Gayla, then snatched a fistful of napkins from the canister on the table. "Now tell me what's wrong," Gertie demanded, pressing the napkins into Gayla's hand.

Although Gayla was tempted, she knew she couldn't share any of her concerns with Gertie. As much as she valued the woman's friendship, she wouldn't burden her with her problems. "It's nothing, really," Gayla replied and sniffed, blotting at her eyes with the napkin.

"Nothing, my foot. I've never seen you cry, other than when Ned died, of course. And God knows, you've had enough to cry over. Now you just empty out your troubles right here on this table and let Gertie have a look at 'em."

Gayla smiled through her tears, thankful for Gertie's

friendship. "It's nothing, really. It's just that I'm so…so happy."

"Happy? This is happy?" Gertie shook her head. "I won't be accepting any such nonsense from you and don't you think you're leaving this diner till I know what's troubling you."

"I love him," Gayla blurted out, then quickly swallowed the sob that rose with the admission.

Gertie looked askance at Gayla. "I would hope you do since you married the man, but is that something to cry over?"

"It is when the love is all one-sided," Gayla replied miserably.

Gertie patted Gayla's hand. "Now, don't you fret over this. Men sometimes don't show their feelings as easily as women. I'm sure he cares for you as much as you do for him."

Gayla shook her head. "No, he doesn't."

"He married you, didn't he? That's the strongest sign of love some men can offer."

Not if the marriage is a lie, Gayla thought sadly. She wanted desperately to unburden herself, to share with Gertie the details of Ned's will and her pact with Brett. But she'd promised, and Gayla never broke a promise. "Gertie?" she asked instead. "How do you make someone fall in love with you?"

Gertie pursed her lips, wagging her head. "Can't," she said without hesitation. "All you can do is offer your heart. It's up to the other person whether they can accept that gift and offer their own in return."

She turned her gaze to the window and a smile

slowly built on her face. "Well, lookee there," Gertie said suddenly, reaching over to poke at Gayla's hand. "Isn't that that good-lookin' husband of yours over there across the street? Wonder where he's going in such a hurry?"

Gayla strained to peer out the window and caught a glimpse of Brett striding down the sidewalk on the opposite side of the street. "I don't know," she murmured, disturbed by Brett's grim expression. When she'd left him, he'd still worn the smile of a satisfied man. Wondering what had happened to change his good mood, she watched until he disappeared into the bank across the street.

Seven

Restless, Brett paced to the window in John Thomas's reception area, shoving his hands deep into his jeans pockets and frowning out at Braesburg's main street. Why he had chosen to seek out John for information concerning his mother and grandfather's relationship, he wasn't sure, but ever since finding the letters in his grandfather's desk the night before, he'd been consumed with the need to know the truth—if there was such a thing. At the moment he was having his doubts.

He'd just decided he was on a fool's mission and had reached for the doorknob, when John stepped from his office. "Sorry to keep you waiting, Brett. What can I help you with?"

Caught before he could make good his exit, Brett

dragged his hand from the knob and slowly turned. "I'm not sure that you can."

"We won't know until you ask." John stepped to the side and gestured for Brett to enter his office. He seated himself behind his desk while Brett took one of the chairs opposite it. "What's on your mind?" John asked as he settled himself comfortably.

Brett frowned. "What do you know about my mother and grandfather's relationship?" he finally asked.

It was John's turn to frown. "I'm not sure what you're asking."

"I want to know what happened between them. Why she left. Yesterday I went over to the hardware store to start cleaning it out. In Ned's office, I found a stack of letters he'd written to my mother that had been returned to him, addressee unknown. My mother was the one who sent them back—I recognized her handwriting." He dragged a hand down the length of his face, the memories of the letters' contents still fresh in his mind. "In the letters, Ned begged for Mother to come home."

John nodded sagely. "I was in law school at the time, but I remember when she left. Ned went crazy. Hired private detectives to track her down."

Brett's frustration grew until it verged on anger. "But Mother always told me that he kicked her out and told her to never return."

John shook his head sadly. "I wasn't present when it happened. No one was but the two of them, but I have a hard time believing Ned would do such a thing.

Hell, he worshiped the ground Christine walked on. Spoiled her rotten. All she had to do was mention she wanted something and it was hers.'' He shook his head again. ''No, I can't believe Ned would have kicked her out. If there were any hard feelings, they were Christine's. Ned loved her and grieved for her till the day he died.''

''Then why?'' Brett cried, slamming his balled fist against the arm of the chair. ''Why would she leave when he was willing to give her anything she wanted just to keep her at home?''

''That's just it. He wasn't able to give her everything. As Christine got older, her demands escalated to the point that Ned almost went broke trying to meet them. When he told her that she was going to have to cut back on her spending a little, she went nuts. Demanded that he sell Parker House and give her the money.''

''And he refused?''

''Yes, though I think it grieved him to have to say no to her.'' He leaned forward, clasping his hands on his desk. ''He was torn between the two people he cared for the most—his wife and his daughter.''

Brett's brow furrowed in confusion. ''But Ned's wife had been dead for years.''

''True, but Parker House was Mrs. Parker's family home. It had been in her family for three generations before she and Ned moved there after her parents passed away. Mrs. Parker had a strong sense of family and tradition. On her deathbed, she made Ned promise that he'd never sell it, but would keep it for Christine.

"Christine knew about her mother's request," John explained further. "She figured the house was hers to do with as she pleased. Ned's refusal to sell the home made her madder than hell."

"Mad enough to leave home and never return?"

John lifted a shoulder. "Who can say? Seems to me she would have been better off staying with Ned instead of striking out on her own. But she was a stubborn girl. Unforgiving."

Brett sat for a moment, absorbing all he'd learned, then stood. He stretched his hand across the width of the desk. "Thanks, John," he murmured. "I appreciate you taking the time to talk to me."

John clasped Brett's hand in his own, his respect for the young man growing by the day. "I'm not sure that I helped you."

Brett let out a weary sigh. "I'm not sure, either. But thanks just the same."

It was late afternoon when Brett returned to Parker House after his visit with John. He went straight to his office and buried himself in paperwork, trying to block out the disturbing things John had told him about his mother.

Although he would have liked to believe otherwise, Brett knew in his heart that the information John had shared with him was the truth. He'd lived with Christine Parker, had been subjected to her unique form of torture—give her what she wanted and you won a smile, cross her and you suffered the lash of her abusive tongue.

From as far back as his memories carried him, he could remember the cruelty of her criticism. Each time he'd displeased her, she had lashed out at him, accusing him of being just like his father—or worse, just like his grandfather. And because Brett knew how much she hated both men, her accusations had cut him to the bone. He'd wanted her love, not her disapproval, so he'd tried harder and harder to please her, but nothing had ever seemed enough.

Brett didn't need a psychologist to probe his psyche to discover the motivation behind his loyalty to his mother. She was all he'd had; it was that damn simple. When his father had moved out when Brett was ten years old, he'd been scared to death that his mother would abandon him, too. So he'd aligned himself with her, striving hard to please her, to make her happy. Nothing he'd ever done had worked.

It wasn't until several years after his father had named him president of Sinclair Corporation that Brett realized that he'd taken his mother's hate for his father and made it his own. The realization had dawned slowly, coming to him as he'd sat by his father's hospital bed and listened while his father had told him his side of their stormy marriage.

But Brett's loyalty to his mother was so ingrained, he had continued to cater to her, just as he'd done all his life.

He rocked back in his chair and dug his fingers through his hair. And what had his loyalty to his mother gotten him? Nothing but a solitary life, the presidency of Sinclair Corporation—where he held no real power—and his grandfather's inheritance. A truckload of problems he could do without.

Except for Gayla.

The thought came unexpectedly, catching Brett off guard, but he slowly conceded it was true.

Without promise of any personal gain, she'd gone along with his marriage scheme so that he could fulfill the stipulations of the will. He suspected her reasons weren't purely altruistic, for he knew she still harbored some hope that in the end Parker House would be saved. But he wouldn't begrudge her that.

Even knowing his plans for Parker House, she continued to work like a slave around the place, getting it ready for guests, stubbornly refusing any offer of payment from him, insisting on continuing to bake for the diner on Main Street for whatever money she needed. So much for his earlier assumption that she was a gold digger, anxious to get her hands on Ned's money.

And she had a kind heart. He'd recognized it first in her affection for Ned, but had grown to admire it more when her kindness was directed at him. And she was more kind than he deserved.

"Brett?"

Gayla's soft voice pulled him from his thoughts. She stood at the office door, poised as if uncertain whether or not she should brave entering his private domain. Her hair fell in fluffy clouds of gold to her shoulders. The faded terry-cloth robe that he had stripped her of that first night cinched her small waist, emphasizing the swell of her breasts and the rounded curves of her hips.

Never had he wanted her more.

"Is it time for bed, already?" he asked, rolling his wrist to look at his watch.

"Yes. I just wanted to remind you to turn down the thermostat. I've already locked the doors."

Was she letting him know in a subtle way that she was planning on sleeping in her own bed, not his? The very thought struck a fearful chord in his heart. He wanted her, needed her with him.

He rose, stretching. "I guess I'll call it a night, too," he said as he rounded his desk. He flipped off the light and followed Gayla out into the hall, stopping only long enough to adjust the thermostat. At the foot of the stairs, Gayla turned toward the hall that led to her room, murmuring a good-night.

Brett caught her hand before she was out of reach. Surprised, she looked up at him. He watched her eyes darken, her cheeks flush, and knew that she wanted him as much as he wanted her. Without a word, he tugged her gently toward him.

Cradling the back of her neck in the width of his hand, he tucked her head beneath his chin, then wrapped his arms around her. He wanted her, but he wouldn't take advantage of her. Not again.

"Twice we've slept together," he murmured against her hair. "Both times offering each other comfort. But I don't need your comfort tonight, Gayla, nor do I think you need mine. I'm not a man who makes promises he knows he won't keep, so I'll not offer any. I want you, Gayla, need you. If that's not enough for you, say so now."

He felt the shudder of emotion that moved through her, sensed her hesitation. He held his breath, fearing that she would say no. He groaned when he felt the tightening of her arms around his waist and the slightest nod of her head against his chest. "It's enough," she whispered.

Stooping to catch her beneath the knees, he lifted her into his arms and climbed the stairs.

The next night, and all that followed, Gayla shared Brett's bed. It was a conscious decision, but not one they discussed again. When bedtime arrived, Brett always sought her out, usually finding her in the kitchen, working. He would help her wind up whatever task she'd been involved in, then take her by the hand and lead her up the stairs to his bed.

They were good together, and good for each other, both needing what the other offered. Brett made no promises to Gayla, and she harbored no doubts that when his six months were up, he still planned to give the estate to the city, file for a divorce and return to Kansas City. Intellectually, Gayla knew this, but convincing her heart of it was an entirely different matter.

Secretly she hoped that Brett would change his mind about Parker House and decide to stay on. She didn't dare let her dreams carry her any further than this, to what would happen between them if he chose to stay. The thought of losing him was simply too painful to consider.

"Gayla!"

Startled from her thoughts, she lifted her head from the depths of the empty hot tub and saw Brett standing on the back porch. "Over here," she called, waving a bleach-soaked rag.

He spotted her, then jogged her way. "What are you up to now?"

"Cleaning out the hot tub. We have a couple scheduled for the carriage house this weekend." She sank back on her heels and tipped her face to the sky. "Isn't this a glorious day?" she murmured appreciatively, closing her eyes and letting the sunshine warm her cheeks.

Having spent the morning in his office with his face lit by the glow of a computer screen, Brett didn't know what kind of day it was. He squinted up at the sky. "Yeah, I guess so," he muttered, already dreading the arrival of the expected guests. He knew it was selfish, but he didn't like sharing Gayla's attention with anyone, preferring to have her all to himself.

Impatiently, he shifted his gaze back to Gayla. "What's for lunch?"

"Is it that time already?" She scrambled to her feet. "I didn't realize how late it was." She quickly gathered her cleaning supplies, but then stopped, letting them fall to the ground. "Let's have a picnic!" she cried, her eyes bright with excitement. "I can throw some things together and we can go down by Town Lake. I know just the spot, too."

Brett didn't have time for a picnic, didn't want to

take the time, for that matter. But Gayla did; he could see it in the hopeful way she looked at him.

"Okay," he grumbled. "But just for an hour. I've work to do."

"An hour, I promise," she pledged, then streaked for the house to pack them a lunch before he could change his mind.

Although he tried his best to remain immune to Gayla's good mood and the sunshiny day, by the end of their picnic lunch, Brett was feeling relaxed and lazy. He lay on his back on the quilt Gayla had spread on the ground, his lightweight jacket wadded beneath his head. He watched puffy clouds drift across a blue sky through the web his eyelashes created and wondered when the seasons had changed.

When he'd first arrived in Braesburg, winter had held the town in its icy clutches. Since then, he'd kept himself holed up in Ned's office and hadn't noticed that spring had made its appearance. Trees had leafed out, flowers had bloomed and the birds had come home to nest. He wondered what else he might have missed out on, if not for Gayla.

"You know what?" he murmured softly.

"What?"

"I've never been on a picnic before."

With the wicker basket between them, Gayla had to sit up to get a look at his face, sure that he was teasing her. "You're kidding."

His head wagged slowly back and forth, his narrowed gaze still focused on the sky overhead. ‘‘Nope. This is my first.’’

She shoved the basket out of the way and pushed up on an elbow in order to see him better. ‘‘But surely when you were young your parents took you on one.’’

‘‘Trust me. I’d remember.’’

Gayla stared at him, saddened because she knew he’d missed out on more than just picnics. She scooted to his side and laid her head on his chest, her hand on his heart.

The action was unexpected and yet so comforting, Brett closed his eyes against the pull of emotion and draped an arm around her shoulders, hugging her to him. Their time together was drawing to an end. In less than three months, he’d have fulfilled his residency requirement and be free to dispose of the estate and return to Kansas City. At the thought, he tightened his arm around her. Already he knew that leaving Gayla would be difficult, but he knew that he couldn’t stay. He had nothing to offer her. Nothing worthwhile, anyway.

Oh, he had plenty of money. As president of Sinclair’s he drew a six-figure salary, plus he had his inheritance from his mother, as well. But Gayla wanted a home, family, roots. Things he couldn’t give her. He’d never known a happy home life, and had no desire to test his own skill at providing one. After all, he was his father’s son…and his mother’s.

Besides, he all but lived out of a suitcase, traveling from store to store, struggling to save Sinclair Corporation from financial ruin. Gayla needed a full-time husband and a passel of children to love and care for. She deserved happiness—something he could never give her.

He lifted his head to plant a kiss on the top of her head, squeezing back the regret that burned in his eyes. She lifted her face and met his gaze. "What was that for?" she asked softly.

He tipped her head back to his chest, not wanting her to see the emotion in his face. "For the picnic," he said, his voice husky. *And for giving me so much,* he added silently.

He wanted desperately to make it up to her. He'd already been toying with an idea and decided this might be the best time to bring it up.

"About those businesses downtown," he began hesitantly.

"What about them?" she asked, trying to keep the hope from her voice.

"I've been thinking. You accused me of being selfish for not sharing my ideas with the other businessmen. More than selfish, I may have been stupid. The hardware store is going to be hell to sell if there isn't any interest in restoring the downtown area, and it looks as if the only way there will be any interest, is if I stir it up myself."

Gayla kept her features schooled. He was lying, and doing a very good job of it. He didn't care one whit whether he sold the hardware store or not. His plan was to give it all to the city, anyway, along with Parker House. For him to show interest in helping to restore the downtown area made Gayla realize that there was still hope of him changing his mind.

"I was thinking the best means of promoting the idea would be to invite all the downtown business owners over one night for a meeting. Since I don't know any of these people, I'll leave the guest list and the inviting up to you."

Gayla felt a lead weight hit the bottom of her stomach. "Me?" she asked halfheartedly.

"Yeah, is that a problem?"

"Well, no," she said slowly. "But I think the people would respond more favorably if the invitation came directly from you, rather than from me."

"Why?"

Gayla's cheeks reddened—and not from exposure to the sun. "I think you are forgetting that I'm Braesburg's version of the Scarlet Woman. I seriously doubt that anyone will accept an invitation from me, no matter what the occasion."

"Do you mind stopping at the grocery store? I need to pick up a few things."

At Gayla's request, Brett whipped into the grocery store's parking lot, still thinking about what Gayla had said. *Braesburg's version of the Scarlet Woman.* She'd lived in the town for nearly ten years, for God's sake. Wouldn't they have either forgotten or forgiven her after that length of time?

Still pensive, he helped her from the truck and let her precede him inside, oblivious to the stares their arrival drew.

But Gayla was aware. And given the fact that during her three-month marriage to Brett, the two of them had never publicly ventured out of the house as a couple, she could almost understand the town's curiosity. Almost.

But she'd heard the rumors around town, the whispered suppositions about her hasty marriage to Ned's grandson. Some claimed she'd married Brett to keep her hand in Ned's pockets, while others were sure she had in some way tricked him into the marriage. Once again, Gayla Matthews was the subject of the town's gossip, the villainess everyone loved to hate.

Let them think what they will, she told herself. She didn't owe the people of Braesburg an explanation and certainly wouldn't offer them more grist for their gossip mill by offering one.

Her chin held high, she grabbed a shopping cart and quickly turned down the first aisle.

"What's the hurry?" Brett asked as he jogged to catch up.

"None," she called over her shoulder. "I just don't want to keep you from your work any longer than necessary."

He caught her elbow, forcing her to a slower pace. "It'll be there when we get home."

Gayla quickly bagged her purchases and headed for the checkout counter. A shopping cart bumped her from the rear and she turned, then stifled a groan when she saw Mabel Pettigrew in line behind her.

"Why, Gayla, is that you?" the woman asked in mock surprise. Before Gayla could respond, Mrs. Pettigrew shifted her gaze to Brett. ''And you must be Gayla's husband, Ned's grandson.''

Brett stuck out his hand. ''Yes, ma'am. Guilty on both counts. I'm Brett Sinclair.''

''Mabel Pettigrew, dear,'' she said, clasping his hand in hers as she gave him a quick once-over. ''I'd heard the two of you had married, but personally didn't believe the gossip. Why, you all couldn't have known each other more than two or three days.''

Brett felt Gayla tense beside him. He slung an arm around Gayla's shoulder, wanting to protect her from any more damaging gossip. ''Couldn't wait any longer,'' he said with a wink at the sour-faced woman. ''Gayla swept me right off my feet.''

Mabel made a clucking sound with her tongue. ''I'd say she did a little more than sweep you off your feet.'' She shifted her gaze to Gayla, arching one eyebrow high and pursing her lips. ''Had the same effect on poor old Ned, God rest his soul.''

''Your total is $23.75, ma'am,'' the cashier interjected.

Gayla flipped open her purse, her fingers trembling as she searched frantically for her wallet. She wanted to get out of the store and away from Mabel Pettigrew's shrewish comments. She'd heard them all before in one form or another, but for Mabel to say these things about her in front of Brett humiliated her beyond anything she'd ever suffered.

Brett closed his hand over hers. ''I'll get it, honey,'' he said softly and squeezed her hand in reassurance. He drew his wallet from his back pocket. ''You know,

Mrs. Pettigrew," he said as he drew two twenties out and tossed them to the clerk, "I've always heard that folks who concern themselves with other people's sex lives do so because they don't have one of their own. Is that true?"

Leaving Mabel standing slack-jawed in line behind him, Brett took his change from the cashier, then grabbed the grocery sack in one hand and Gayla in the other. With a quick nod in the cashier's direction, he guided Gayla out of the store.

Once inside his truck, Gayla sat, her spine board straight and her gaze locked on the windshield. "That wasn't necessary," she said, her voice tight with carefully controlled emotion.

"Neither were the things she said," Brett replied angrily. "They weren't true and certainly weren't fair."

"No, they weren't. But do you really think you helped things any by insulting her? In less than three months, you'll file for a divorce, and leave Braesburg and all the gossip behind." She turned slowly, pinning him with her gaze. "But I'll still be here, Brett. What do you think Mrs. Pettigrew will have to say then?"

Gayla's comment haunted Brett. She was right. He would be gone in less than three months and she would be left to face all the questions alone. He hadn't thought about that when he'd come up with the scheme for them to marry, but then he'd assumed that Gayla would be as anxious to leave Braesburg as he.

He couldn't forget, either, the condemnation in Mrs.

Pettigrew's accusations and the condescending tone she'd used when referring to Gayla. It made him all too aware that Gayla might be right in her assumption that no one in Braesburg would accept an invitation from her to attend a meeting at Parker House.

But they would. Brett would see to that.

He called John Thomas and the Reverend Brown and asked them to meet him at Gertie's Diner on Main Street for a cup of coffee. They all arrived at the same time, and Brett ushered them to a rear booth, hoping for a bit of privacy.

Once their coffee mugs were filled by the waitress, Brett didn't waste any time. "I need your help," he said, and quickly reviewed his plans for the renovation of the downtown area, winning nods of approval from both men. He then told them that he had decided to launch the idea at a meeting he was calling with several of the owners of downtown buildings. "The problem is Gayla," he finished, frowning. "She thinks no one will come because of her."

John and the reverend exchanged a look. Both turned their gazes on their coffee cups. The reverend shook his head sadly. "Much as I hate to admit it about my own parishioners, I think Gayla is right. No one will even consider accepting an invitation from her."

Brett shifted his gaze to John. John lifted a shoulder in a shrug, but shook his head as well. "I'm afraid I agree with Reverend Brown."

"But why?" Brett asked in disbelief.

"This is a small town," John replied. "Quick to

make assumptions, slow to forget, slower still to forgive.'' He shook his head. ''Gayla's mother's reputation wasn't the best, then when she moved off and left Gayla with Ned... Well, folks just assumed the worst.'' He frowned. ''Ned didn't help things. Stubborn old cuss. Rather than deny the rumors, he let them spread until they took on a life of their own.''

Brett sagged against the booth with a weary sigh. ''Damn it,'' he said and slapped an open palm to the Formica tabletop. ''That's not fair. Gayla never did anything to deserve their scorn.''

John lifted an eyebrow, looking pointedly at Brett. ''You haven't done much to change their opinion.''

Brett knew John was right. After his conversation with Mabel Pettigrew, Brett was only too aware how much speculation his marriage to Gayla had caused, and all to Gayla's detriment. ''No,'' he murmured morosely. ''I guess I haven't. But I want to change that—at least as much as I can.'' He leaned forward, catching his mug between his hands. ''And that's why I asked you to meet me here, instead of at the house. I don't want Gayla to know anything about this.'' He pulled a copy of the guest list from his pocket and laid it on the table in front of them. ''These are the people that Gayla's planning to invite. You know them. I want you to do whatever you can to persuade them to come to Parker House for the meeting.''

''And this is going to change the town's opinion of Gayla?'' John asked doubtfully.

Brett drew in a deep breath. ''No, but it's a start.''

* * *

The following week was a nightmare of activity. Brett might have had the ideas for the renovation of downtown Braesburg, but he drew Gayla into the preparations. They photographed the existing downtown area and enlarged the prints for demonstration purposes. He had Gayla dig through the historical society's badly kept records, looking for photos that pictured the downtown area in its prime.

He poured through travel brochures, seeking out small towns that had implemented a similar marketing scheme with successful results. Once he'd gathered all the information he thought he would need, he made copies and compiled a folder for each guest.

Meanwhile, Gayla issued invitations to six of the owners of downtown buildings and their wives and prayed, for Brett's sake, that they would accept.

The night of the meeting arrived and with it a bad case of nerves for Gayla. Deciding the living room provided a more relaxed setting than the dining room, she opted to seat her guests there—if they showed up at all. She covered the library table with Mrs. Parker's Battenberg lace cloth, and set out a variety of desserts. While the coffee brewed, filling the living room with the rich aroma of Irish cream-flavored coffee, she arranged the chairs, placing on each one of the folders she and Brett had prepared. Angling the frame to the best advantage, she stood the easel with the flip charts Brett had prepared in the curve of the grand piano.

The doorbell rang and Gayla whirled, already wringing her hands at her waist. Brett stuck his head into the living room. "I believe the guests you swore wouldn't come are arriving,'' he said, teasing her with that half smile.

''Yes, I guess they are,'' she murmured, suddenly feeling sick at her stomach. ''Do you mind if I wait in the kitchen? You can call me if you need anything.''

Brett stepped into the living room, wagging his head. ''And miss all the fun?'' He caught her hand and slipped it through the crook of his arm. ''Besides, I need you to introduce me to all these people.''

Gayla went with him and forced a smile as she opened the front door. Of all people, Mabel Pettigrew stood at the threshold. Brett saw Gayla's hesitation and placed a reassuring hand on her shoulder. He reached around Gayla, extending his hand in greeting to Mabel. ''Mrs. Pettigrew,'' he said politely. ''I'm so glad you could join us.'' He angled himself to include the man beside her in the greeting, and couldn't help wondering if Mabel had told her husband about their conversation in the grocery store. ''And you must be Mr. Pettigrew.'' At the man's curt nod, Brett said, ''I've heard a lot about you from Gayla. She tells me that you owned one of the finest furniture stores in the county.'' Mr. Pettigrew frowned, but stole a quick glance at Gayla.

A second couple climbed the porch steps, quickly followed by a third. Gayla couldn't disguise her surprise. She introduced each of them to Brett—the Baxters, the Colliers, the Masons, the Broussards and the Grants. Although none were overly friendly, they had at least responded to her invitation. For that courtesy alone, Gayla would forever be in their debt.

She guided them into the living room and to the refreshment table, then invited them to sit down. Just as she was about to take a seat herself, the doorbell chimed again. Puzzled, she crossed quickly to the entrance and opened the door. In front of her stood none other than Mary Frances Farnsley, the self-proclaimed First Lady of Braesburg. Gayla hadn't invited Mary Frances and didn't know what to say, but Mary Frances saved her any awkwardness.

"I hope I'm not too late," Mary Frances fretted as she boldly stepped inside. "I had to take Peaches, my dog, over to Miss Singer's. Peaches hates to stay at the house by herself when I'm away." Her eyes darting about, she spied the guests in the living room and headed that way, the soles of her crepe-soled walking shoes squeaking on the hardwood floor. Gayla followed, unsure what to do with this uninvited guest.

Mary Frances seized a plate and piled on desserts. Gayla tried hard not to laugh at the woman's audacity as she poured her a cup of coffee. Brett walked over. "I don't believe I've had the pleasure," he said, offering his hand to the new arrival. "I'm Brett Sinclair."

Mary Frances grabbed his hand and pumped. "Mary Frances Farnsley," she replied briskly. "I'm the mayor's wife."

Although her husband hadn't served as mayor in over twenty years, Mary Frances still considered herself the First Lady of Braesburg. No one had the nerve to challenge her on the issue, for although she was eccentric, Mary Frances was harmless and was dedicated to Braesburg's welfare.

She took a seat close to the front and gestured with her fork for Brett to get on with the meeting.

He didn't appear the least bit nervous, but Gayla's stomach continued to do a series of somersaults as she slipped into a chair at the rear of the room. Gayla couldn't stop the swell of pride that surged as she watched Brett move through the web of chairs to stand before the group. He looked so handsome, and she couldn't deny the thrill of pleasure that shot through her. Ned would be so proud, she thought. His own grandson, heading up a committee to save the downtown area of Braesburg.

"Before I begin," Brett said, "I'd like to thank all of you for taking time out of your own busy schedules to come here tonight. I'm sure that some of you come as doubters, others with your minds already made up, unwilling to invest another penny in properties that have already cost you more in taxes than they are currently worth."

He shifted his gaze from one frowning face to another, until he'd met every skeptical look in the room. "But my purpose tonight is to change your minds." He paced the length of the grand piano and back. "I'm not a longtime resident of Braesburg," he said. "I don't have the history or the experience with this town that most of you in the room possess." He stopped and leveled his gaze on them. "But my interests equal yours, as I, too, own property downtown."

Gayla's breath was lodged somewhere between her lungs and throat. What a stroke of genius! Instead of avoiding any objections the property owners might have, he'd voiced them himself, thus weakening their effectiveness in an argument. If Gayla had harbored any doubts of Brett's ability to unite these people, the delivery of his opening alone would have convinced her.

She listened, enraptured, as he built his case, showing the present condition of the downtown area, comparing its buildings with the original photographs. He plied them with statistics of other communities that had revamped their downtown areas and experienced a surge in revenues. To cap it all off, he threw transparencies over the old photographs, superimposing his own interpretation of the downtown area after renovation.

Having given them every argument he could think of, Brett laid aside the pointer he had used throughout the presentation. "Are there any questions?" he asked.

No one looked at him or said a word. Not one of them. They kept their heads down, their gazes averted. With the exception of Mary Frances Farnsley. She twisted in her chair, this way and that, waiting for someone to speak up. When it became apparent they wouldn't, she jumped to her feet and faced them. "What's wrong with you people? Are you deaf? The man has just given you the solution to our problems and you're all sitting there like a bunch of bullfrogs on a log."

Old man Pettigrew raised his head, glaring at Mary

Frances. ''Easy for you to say, Mary Frances. You don't have anything invested here.''

She whipped around to Brett. ''There are common areas, aren't there? Places you'll be needing someone other than the property owners to take care of?''

''Yes, ma'am,'' Brett replied, indicating a strip down the center of the main street where park benches and shade trees were depicted.

''I'll take care of that.'' Mary Frances flopped down in her chair and dug out a well-worn checkbook from her handbag. ''I'll start the beautification fund with a thousand dollars,'' she said as she wrote out the check. ''And I'll personally be responsible for raising any more capital that is needed.''

She flung the check out to Brett, then turned to glare at the others. ''Well, now, what have you got to say?''

Mrs. Grant who had a tendency to whine, did so now. ''We're too old to start over again. What little money we've set aside is for our retirement. We can't afford to gamble away our life's savings.''

Mary Frances silenced her with a glare. ''You're old when you can't find anyone around older than yourself, and I happen to know that I'm a good five years older than you, Millie Grant. So, as long as I'm alive, you aren't old.''

Ted Baxter spoke up. ''It's not my age I'm worried about. It's the money that concerns me. I haven't got it and I don't believe the bank will be willing to make a note on anything as risky as this.'' Others murmured their agreement.

Brett stepped forward. ''I'll loan you the money,

and anyone else who's willing to take a chance with me. Ten thousand dollars, interest free, with no payments due for five years. So, what do you say? Do I have any takers?"

Gayla couldn't believe her ears. Could this mean that Brett was planning on staying in Braesburg beyond his six-month requirement?

No, she warned herself and placed a hand against her thudding heart. *Don't set yourself up for disappointment. He's a businessman closing a deal. Nothing more.* But she kept her hand over her heart, which threatened to pound right through her chest as she watched Ted Baxter stand and offer Brett his hand.

Eight

Gayla closed the door behind the last guest. Then, unable to contain her excitement any longer, she whirled and launched herself into Brett's arms. "You did it!" she cried, laughing and hugging him. "You really did it!"

"Don't count your chickens before they're hatched," he warned, trying to keep his own excitement in check. "Only two of the six agreed to join in with the renovations. And the credit's not all mine," he added, tipping her chin up and smiling down into her face. "You deserve a share."

Gayla flattened her hands against his chest. "No, it was you," she argued. "All the ideas, the strategies, the concept, everything! It was all you." She looped her hands behind his neck. "Oh, Brett, Ned would have been so proud."

The idea of his grandfather being proud of him was still a hard pill for Brett to swallow, but he wouldn't ruin Gayla's excitement. Not tonight.

"I think this calls for a celebration," he said. "Don't you?"

"Definitely. There's a bottle of champagne in the refrigerator. I'll get it."

She spun out of his arms, but Brett caught her before she could escape. "How about if I get the champagne and you grab a couple of towels and we meet out at the hot tub?"

Gayla's eyes widened, her heart thrummed in her chest. "Okay," she replied a little breathlessly.

"Oh, and Gayla," Brett called before she made it to the kitchen door. "Don't bother with a swimsuit."

Like the champagne, the night was cool and filled with magic. Stars winked on and off through the lacy canopy of foliage above the hot tub while a quarter moon played a game of hide-and-seek between the tree's branches.

Gayla stood at the side of the hot tub, her terry robe wrapped tightly around her, hugging the bottle of champagne and two fluted glasses to her breasts. Beneath her robe, she was as naked as the day she was born. That knowledge alone drew a blush to her cheeks and a fever to her skin. She'd never felt so wanton in her life.

Setting the bottle and glasses on the tub's ledge, she

leaned over to test the water's temperature. Steam misted her cheeks, adding to the heat that already pulsed through her. Brett brushed past her, adjusting the controls on the tub. Nerves skittered beneath her skin at his brief touch.

Before she could recover, he was behind her, his hands resting on her shoulders, his lips pressed to her ear. He eased the robe from her shoulders and the cool night air hit her fevered skin, making her shiver. He circled her waist with his arms and drew her back against him, dipping his knees to fit his body against her curves. "Cold?" he murmured at her ear.

"A little," she replied breathlessly.

"The water will warm you up," he promised and guided her up the steps and into the tub.

While she sank beneath the churning water and settled herself on the bench, Brett shed his own clothes. Moonlight added a level of intimacy to the act that their bedroom lacked. Like a voyeur, Gayla watched.

His body was familiar to her, almost as familiar as her own. The broad shoulders, muscled arms and legs. The dark hair that covered his chest and tickled her nose when she snuggled against him. The scar on his right shoulder blade he bore as the result of a motorcycle wreck in his teens.

He glanced up and caught her watching. Grinning, he swung a leg over the edge and eased into the tub opposite her. The water churned and bubbled around him, quickly covering his nakedness. Gayla's pent-up breath came out in a lustful sigh.

He popped the cork on the champagne bottle, filled

the glasses, and passed Gayla hers. He lifted his in a toast. "To Braesburg," he said, then leaned to tap his glass gently against Gayla's.

"To Braesburg," she concurred and took a cautious sip. She wrinkled her nose, laughing as the bubbles tickled her upper lip. Still high from the night's successes, she propped her feet on the bench beside Brett and shook back her hair. She took a long drink of the champagne, then wiggled her toes in the frothy water. "This is absolutely decadent."

That simple statement told Brett a great deal about Gayla's life experiences up to this point. Wanting to add to her enjoyment, he set his champagne glass aside, picked up her foot and began to massage her arch.

"Hmm," she murmured appreciatively. "That feels wonderful." She drew the champagne glass to her forehead. "I can feel it all the way up here."

"The champagne?" he asked, teasing her.

She laughed. "No, silly. Whatever it is you're doing to my foot. It's sending little pulses of sensation all the way to my head." She took another sip of champagne, then rested it on the edge of the tub, spilling a little of the golden liquid. Brett wondered if she was getting a little tipsy.

She sat for a moment, studying him. "Is there anyone in Kansas City waiting for you to return home?"

His hands stilled on her foot as he looked across the churning water at her. This was the first time she'd ever asked about his personal life. "Where did that come from?"

"Just curious."

He curled his fingers around her foot and continued the massage. "No. How about you?"

"Me?" Gayla laughed, then hiccuped. Pressing her fingertips against her lips, she giggled, then replied very primly, "You know very well that there isn't anyone."

"Not ever?"

"You'll find this hard to believe, especially with the reputation I have in this town, but I haven't even had so much as a date in years."

Brett looked at her in amazement. "Surely you've had boyfriends?"

Gayla sipped thoughtfully at the champagne. "Once. Years ago, the summer after I graduated from high school." She sighed and slipped lower in the tub until the water reached her chin. "I thought I was in love. Lost my virginity in the back seat of his daddy's car." Her eyes took on a faraway look.

"What happened?"

Slowly, Gayla focused on Brett's face. "He dumped me." She lifted the glass to her lips and drained it. "I made the mistake of telling him I loved him and—poof!—he was gone." She stretched to snag the bottle of champagne. "I was so naive," she added with a rueful shake of her head as she refilled her glass. "I thought that because we'd made love that it meant he loved me. It didn't and he didn't. Since he, along with everyone else in town, thought I was Ned's mistress, he assumed that I wouldn't mind spreading a little around. He even thought I'd be grateful, considering how Ned was such an old man.''

It was obvious that Gayla had been hurt. And how anyone would want to hurt someone as kind as Gayla, Brett couldn't fathom. ''The son of a bitch,'' he muttered, wanting to close his hands around the guy's neck and squeeze for treating her feelings so carelessly.

Gayla grinned a little lopsidedly. ''He was, wasn't he?'' She lifted her glass in a toast to Brett. ''Here's to all the sons of bitches in the world.'' She tipped up the glass and drained it.

Brett frowned. ''Maybe you'd better go easy on the champagne.''

''Why?'' she asked, and hiccuped again.

''I don't think you're used to drinking this much.''

She crooked her index finger, motioning for him to lean forward. ''I'll tell you a little secret,'' she said in a stage whisper at his ear. ''I never drink.'' She fell back against the side of the hot tub, laughing.

Brett shook his head, chuckling. Yep, she was drunk.

Her laughter slowly faded into a deep sigh, her gaze settling on him. Her eyes darkened, taking on a smoky hue. ''Are you done with that massage yet?'' she asked, her voice husky.

He stilled his fingers. ''Well, sure. I guess.''

''Good.''

Surprised, he looked at her. ''Good? But I thought you were enjoying it?''

''I was.'' She tossed the champagne glass over her

shoulder and didn't even flinch when it shattered on the flagstone patio behind her. "But now I want to celebrate."

She dragged her foot from his grasp, then slipped beneath the water. Startled, Brett started to grab for her, scared that she would drown herself. Before he could move, she resurfaced at his knees. She rose like a siren from the deep, lifting her arms to smooth her hair from her face while water sluiced down her body and dripped off her breasts.

Smiling seductively, she looped her arms around his neck, and wiggled until she'd managed to straddle his thighs. Water continued to churn and steam around them, adding a mystical quality to the night. Catching his cheeks between her hands, she angled his face toward hers, then closed her mouth over his.

Gayla, the seductress. Brett smiled against her lips. What had happened to the shy, somewhat reserved woman he'd first made love with? He knew the champagne had a lot to do with her current boldness, but he knew, too, that she was growing more sure of herself and her sexuality with every passing day.

Every passing day... He tightened his arms around her at the unwanted reminder. The days were passing. Faster and faster, with a disregard for his sudden need for them to slow down. When he'd first heard the terms of Ned's will, six months had seemed like an eternity, but now he found himself wishing Ned had required an even lengthier residency requirement.

Wanting to hold on to this moment, he wrapped his arms around Gayla and drew her closer until the swell of his manhood nested against her femininity. He held her tight, his heart full of conflicting emotions, wanting this night never to end.

But Gayla was oblivious to his need to go slow. The champagne had robbed her of any inhibitions. Purring like a cat, she bent backwards from the waist, arching against his hands, drawing his face to the breasts she thrust temptingly before him. At the invitation, he closed his lips over one turgid nipple, drawing it deep into his mouth. She groaned as hot arrows of sensation shot through her to stab at the very center of her. The water churning around them only added to the sensual pleasures pulsing within her. Savoring the feelings that ebbed around her, she wrapped her legs around his waist, teasing herself with the pressure of his arousal until she couldn't stand the anticipation any longer.

Rising to her knees, she guided him to her, then slowly eased back down until he was buried deep within her. She closed her lips over his, absorbing the groan of pleasure that welled from deep within him. Slowly she leaned back again, dragging her mouth from his, keeping him inside her, but adding a new angle, a new pressure to their joining.

Steam rose in clouds around them, pearling their bodies with beads of moisture as the water churned. Unable to hold back any longer, Brett caught her hips between his hands. He drove his body against hers, faster and faster, burying himself deeper and deeper with each new thrust. He caught her hard against him as pleasure peaked, curling into a hard, tight ball within him, then exploding in a wild burst of color behind his closed eyes.

Bonelessly, he melted against her, her name on his lips as he gathered her close to his heart.

Gayla stood on the sidewalk, the handle of a picnic basket gripped in one hand and a jug of lemonade in the other while she searched for Brett in the crowd of workers. As she spotted him, a smile curved her lips. He stood at the top of a ladder, his chest bare, a yellow hard hat perched at a cocky angle on his head. A leather tool belt rode low on his hips and sweat darkened a half-moon at the waist of his faded jeans. Gayla's cheeks puffed in a lustful sigh.

He couldn't have looked any more sexy if he'd been stripped naked and sprawled on satin sheets.

Sighing again, she pushed through the crowd of workmen until she reached the ladder where he worked. "Hey, handsome," she called up to him. "How about a break?"

He glanced down, and she lifted the basket and the jug. He shot her a wink and a grin and started down the ladder. Gayla stood below enjoying the way the muscles in his butt tightened and relaxed with each downward step. By the time his boot hit the sidewalk, her mouth was as dry as sandpaper and her palms damp with perspiration.

He grinned. She smiled. Then, right there in front of God and everybody, he dipped his head over hers, momentarily blocking out the sun as he pressed a kiss onto her waiting lips. He tasted like sweat and hard work and sunshine, and Gayla knew if she lived to be a hundred she would never forget that unique blend of flavors. She leaned into him, wanting to get closer, but hampered by the things she held in her hands.

Brett grinned against her lips. "Lusty little devil, aren't you?" he murmured and cupped his hands around her buttocks, squeezing her to him briefly, before withdrawing.

Gayla smiled coyly. "I've been called worse." She gestured to one of the new park benches gracing the tree-lined median that ran the length of Main Street. "How about lunch?" she asked. "We can grab some shade under those trees."

Brett snagged the handle of the picnic basket from her hand, then caught her by the elbow and guided her across the street. He slid the basket onto the bench, then flipped open the lid. "What did you bring?" he asked, already digging. "I'm famished."

"Fried chicken, coleslaw, deviled eggs, fruit." She slapped his hand when he dipped his finger into the icing on the chocolate cake. "Hey, that's for dessert."

He popped his finger into his mouth and sank onto the bench, catching her hand and tugging her down beside him as he sucked the rich chocolate off his finger. "Woman, you sure know how to please a man."

Gayla couldn't help but smile. "Flattery will get you everywhere," she said, teasing him. Tipping the jug, she poured a glass of lemonade, then passed it to him. While he drank, she looked around, admiring all the changes that had occurred over the last two months.

Her eyes widened when she caught a glimpse of a man farther down the block, dressed in overalls and pushing a wheelbarrow filled with debris. "Brett!" she cried, pointing. "Look! Isn't that Ed Pettigrew?"

Brett followed the line of her finger. "Yep, that's Ed, all right," he said, grinning.

"But I thought he was totally opposed to the renovation."

Brett nodded. "He was. But he's been hanging around lately, kind of checking things out. Said he liked the way things were shaping up. He's helping Ted clear out his store for now, but I think before it's over, Ted'll have to return the favor."

Gayla fell back against the bench, her jaw still sagging open. "I can't believe it," she murmured.

"Believe it," Brett replied with a teasing smile. "After all, you are the force behind the change."

"Me?"

Brett nodded and picked up a chicken leg. "If not for you, I would never have met with these people and this whole project would never have materialized."

Although Gayla knew her part was small, Brett's praise pleased her enormously. "Oh, you're just saying that because I brought you lunch," she said, trying to make light of it.

"No, it's true," Brett argued. Grinning, he hooked an arm along the back of the park bench and put his mouth close to her ear. "And just think. If we hadn't encouraged these folks to get out and do something about the downtown area, poor old Ed would still be sitting at home listening to prune-faced Mabel harp about how wonderful and sinfully exciting our sex life is."

Laughing, Gayla plucked a plump strawberry from the basket. Holding it by its stem, she teased him with a coy look. "You wish," she said, then stuffed the strawberry into Brett's mouth, laughing.

"My, what a lovely home you have," Fay Cummings murmured appreciatively, looking around while her husband signed the guest register.

Although she knew Parker House was not truly hers, Gayla accepted the compliment with a smile. "Thanks, we like it."

Roger Cummings straightened, tucking his pen back into his shirt pocket. "As we were driving in, I noticed all the construction downtown. What's going on?"

"A face-lift," Gayla said, closing the register. "If you're interested, I can show you the plans." At Roger's nod, she gestured for them to follow her into the living room where the easel holding the sketches for the final plan still stood in the curve of the grand piano. She stepped to the side while the Cummingses studied the drawings. "The property owners have banded together and are restoring all the buildings on Main Street to their original fronts," Gayla explained. "It's going to be quite impressive when they're done."

Roger nodded his agreement. "It certainly is." He pulled off his glasses and tucked them into his shirt pocket. ''Do you suppose it would be all right if we went down for a closer look?''

''I'm sure it would be fine. In fact, my husband is down there working right now. He'd be more than happy to give you a tour. If you'd like, I could drive you down there now myself and introduce you.''

''We wouldn't want to be any trouble,'' Roger said.

''No trouble. I go down every afternoon and take the men something cool to drink. Just follow me,'' she said, and led them out to her car.

When she slipped into a parking space on Main Street, a group of men descended on her car. Laughing, Gayla jumped out and unlocked her trunk. ''Did you think I wasn't coming?'' she teased as she lifted the trunk lid. She stepped back, allowing George and Finley, two of the workers, access to the drinks she'd iced down. After they'd removed the cooler, she drew out a box of cookies she'd baked that morning. She handed the box to Ted Baxter, who stood waiting. ''Now you have to share,'' Gayla scolded good-naturedly.

''As if I have a choice,'' Ted replied dryly and slapped Finley's hand from the box.

Laughing, Gayla turned to search for Brett. It didn't take long. Shirtless, he stood out like a beacon among the other workers. Waving her hand above her head to get his attention, she wove her way through the equipment and materials cluttering the sidewalk, with the Cummingses following close behind. When she reached Brett's side, she rose on tiptoe to give him a quick kiss. ''Hi,'' she murmured, licking the salty taste of his perspiration from her lips.

Brett watched the seductive play of her tongue and groaned. ''Hi, yourself,'' he said and gathered her in his arms, ready to claim a more intimate kiss. He stopped when he noticed the older couple standing behind Gayla, watching.

Gayla turned, angling herself to include the Cummingses. ''Brett, I'd like for you to meet our houseguests for the weekend, Roger and Fay Cummings. Roger and Fay, this is my husband, Brett Sinclair.''

My husband, Brett Sinclair. The attribute wasn't one Brett had heard Gayla use before, but before he could decide if he liked the sound of it or not, Roger Cummings was extending his hand in greeting while Gayla explained, ''The Cummingses are interested in seeing the renovation and I thought maybe you could give them a tour.''

Brett nabbed his shirt from the tailgate of his truck and shrugged it on. ''Sure. I'd be happy to.''

Taking Gayla's hand, Brett led the way down the street, pointing out the changes that had already been implemented, and explaining those that still remained to be made. Gayla heard the pride in his voice, saw the enthusiasm that lit his eyes and felt her heart tighten in her chest.

The changes going on in Braesburg weren't all centered in the downtown area. Brett Sinclair was going through a pretty spectacular metamorphosis himself. She wondered if he realized just how much he'd changed since he'd begun work on the downtown project. She never caught him gulping milk in the middle of the night to ease his ulcer anymore, he rarely threw temper tantrums, and he smiled almost all the time. She knew that he found his current work a hundred times more satisfying than his job as president of Sinclair's. She wished with all her heart that he would realize that, too. There was still time, she told herself.

As they walked, Brett stopped now and then to discuss something with some of the other men still working. When they approached the Masons' store, Clara Mason was out sweeping wood shavings into a neat pile on the sidewalk. At the sight of Gayla and Brett, she paused in her sweeping. She glanced at their joined hands, then back to Gayla, offering a shy smile.

''Good afternoon, Gayla, Brett,'' she said as they passed by.

Gayla nearly fell out of her socks. Clara Mason had been one of the committee of three who had visited Ned, voicing their disapproval when Gayla had moved in with him. In the ten years that Gayla had lived in Braesburg, the woman had never given her so much as the time of day, except to snub her nose when their paths crossed. Unable to believe this change of heart, Gayla stammered in return, ''G-good afternoon, Mrs. Mason.''

And Clara Mason wasn't the only person Gayla noticed looking her way. Polite nods came from nearly everyone they met on the street. The same people who had ignored her for years, were now being polite?

Gayla swallowed back the wad of emotion that rose to her throat. For years she'd spouted that the citizens of Braesburg's opinion of her didn't matter. But it had. Silently, in her heart of hearts, she had wanted their acceptance. She tightened her fingers around Brett's, sure that in some way he had played a part in this change.

Unaware of her thoughts, he glanced down at her, smiling, and squeezed her hand in return before leading the Cummingses into the old hardware store.

"Brett," Gayla whispered. "Are you asleep?"

"Not anymore," he murmured and rolled onto his back.

"I'm sorry," she said in apology, and leaned to smooth his hair from his forehead so she could press a kiss there. "But something has been bothering me all day."

"What?"

"I know this probably sounds silly, but everyone around town seems to be acting nicer toward me and I wondered if you'd noticed."

Brett chuckled. "Of course, they're being nice to you. You bring them cold drinks and cookies every day."

Her expression fell and Brett immediately regretted teasing her. "Hey," he said tenderly, tipping up her chin. "I was just kidding with you." In the moonlight that filtered through the lace curtains, he caught the glimmer of tears in her eyes. "Ah, honey," he said and pulled her close. "Don't cry. It doesn't matter what those people think of you."

Gayla shook her head. "Yes, it does." She swiped at a stray tear with the tip of her finger. "I used to try to convince myself it didn't matter, but it does and always has. But for some reason, since we started working on the project downtown, it seems as if everyone is...well, nicer."

Brett could see how important this was to her. "They're getting to know you," he said softly. "In time, all those old rumors will be forgotten."

She rolled onto her back, her shoulder touching Brett's as she stared at the shadowed ceiling. "I hope so," she said with a sigh. She reached for his hand and laced her fingers through his. "Thanks, Brett."

The sweetness of her fingers wound through his and the total trust of the gesture, drew a lump to Brett's throat. He knew he didn't deserve this woman—not even for the short time that she was his.

Normally, when Parker House was booked, Gayla served her guests breakfast in the garden room and ate her own meal with Brett in the kitchen. But the Cummingses had requested that she and Brett join them for breakfast. They were such nice people and such good company, Gayla had agreed. She set the table for four and prepared everything buffet-style to make the meal more relaxing for everyone.

"What did you do before you retired, Roger?" Brett asked.

"I was a city planner."

Brett's eyes widened in interest. "We could sure use some of your expertise around here."

Roger and Fay shared a glance. Roger cleared his throat. "Fay and I were thinking the same thing. Not that you people haven't done a tremendous job with your renovation. But this is just the beginning. Businesses have to be opened, a marketing strategy devised. Everything needs to follow a common theme in order to guarantee success. Fay, here," he continued, giving her hand an affectionate pat, "has always wanted to own a retail shop. What with the children gone and me retired, we now have the opportunity and the funds to chase a few dreams." He cleared his throat again. "To get to the point. We were wondering if you'd be interested in selling us the hardware store."

Gayla tried to keep her food down and her face free of emotion. *Sell the hardware store?* Would Brett do it? she wondered. In a matter of weeks, he would have fulfilled his six-month residency requirement and be free to dispose of any part of Ned's estate that he wanted. Including Parker House. It was that thought that struck the deepest chord of fear within her.

She'd hoped that his involvement with the renovation project would draw him closer to Braesburg, to his heritage and the house that was so much a part of that heritage. But had it? She didn't dare look at him, for fear he would guess her thoughts, her fears. *Oh, God, please,* she silently begged. *Don't let him sell out. Not yet.*

"I don't know," Brett replied hesitantly. "I haven't given the idea of selling the place enough thought to even put a price on it."

"No rush," Roger assured him. "Fay and I are going to be traveling throughout the Southwest for the next month or so. We'll stop back on our way home." He looked over the top of his bifocals at Brett. "But if you do decide to sell, we'd like first option."

Gayla collapsed inwardly, feeling as if she'd won a reprieve, no matter how short.

Gayla stood at the sink, rinsing the breakfast dishes. Through the kitchen window she watched Brett on the driveway outside helping the Cummingses load their suitcases into the trunk of their car. Roger handed him a business card and she saw Brett glance at it briefly before tucking it into his shirt pocket. Knowing that they were making plans to further discuss the Cummingses desire to purchase the hardware store, she turned away, unable to watch.

The back door opened and closed, and the scrape of Brett's boots sounded on the tile floor as he made his way toward her. He stepped up behind her and wrapped his arms around her waist, matching the length of his body to hers. "Alone at last," he whispered against her ear.

Gayla's lips curved in a halfhearted smile, but she kept her hands in the dishwater to hide her nerves. Brett caught the lobe of her ear between his teeth. "Nice people," he murmured, "but I'm sure glad they're gone."

"That was some surprise," Gayla said, trying hard to keep the quiver from her voice, "Roger offering to buy the hardware store, and all."

''Uh-huh,'' Brett mumbled in disinterest.

''Do you think you'll sell it to him?''

The tremor in her voice slowly registered, and Brett turned her around to face him. ''Would it matter to you if I did?'' he asked.

With the thought of losing him pressing on her heart, looking at him, at the features so much like Ned's, that she had grown to cherish over the last months—was almost too painful to bear. Blue eyes that turned dark and stormy in passion, were now filled with concern.

Matter? she asked herself. Only if it meant losing him, but she couldn't tell him that. She dipped her chin, unable to meet the intensity of his blue eyes. ''No,'' she murmured, knowing it was a partial lie. ''Though I had hoped if you decided to stay, you might open your own business there.''

Brett's forehead wrinkled in a frown. ''Stay?'' he repeated. ''In Braesburg?'' When she didn't look at him, he felt the blood drain from his limbs. ''Gayla, honey,'' he said, trying to be gentle. ''I told you from the first. I'm not staying in Braesburg. My home, my business is in Kansas City.''

She dug her fingernails into her palms. She wouldn't cry, she told herself. That would only make things worse. She kept her gaze down until she knew she had the tears under control, then lifted her head and tossed back her hair. ''I know,'' she said, forcing a breezy smile. ''I just thought that you might. You know, since you seemed to really enjoy working on the renovation, and all.''

"That's true," he admitted carefully, not wanting to foster any false hope. "I have enjoyed the work. But my responsibilities lie with Sinclair's. I've wasted enough time down here, as it is."

Two weeks. Fourteen short days. Gayla caught her lower lip between her teeth as she stared at the kitchen calendar and fought back tears. She'd always known that Brett intended to leave Braesburg; he'd never pretended anything else. But at some point over the past months, she'd allowed herself to dream, to hope that he would change his mind about Parker House and decide to stay. As foolish as it now seemed, she had actually let herself believe that they were husband and wife in the truest sense of the word.

But his announcement stripped Gayla of every thread of hope that she'd fostered and left her feeling empty and alone.

Not yet, you're not, she told herself, giving herself a firm shake. *You have two weeks with him. And by God they'll be happy ones.*

Nine

Gayla sat hunched over the lunch counter at Gertie's Diner, a copy of the Austin *American Statesman* spread beneath her elbows. She quickly scanned the half-page story, while Gertie looked on, smiling smugly. The headline read: Sinclair's Corporate President Gives Braesburg New Lease On Life. A second headline hinted: Corporate Headquarters Move In Near Future? Pictures of the current construction accompanied the text, which speculated on Brett's involvement in Braesburg, drawing questions about his possible intent to move Sinclair's headquarters from Kansas City to the small Texas town. Copies of the *Dallas Morning News* and the *Houston Post,* carrying similar stories, lay on the floor where Gayla had dropped them in her excitement.

Gayla glanced up, meeting Gertie's smiling eyes. "I can't believe this," she murmured, wondering if there was any truth to the speculation.

"Nobody can," Gertie replied. "Madge over at the Chamber office says the phone's been ringing off the wall. Some of 'em are folks calling just to see if it's true, but others are interested in putting in businesses."

Gayla sagged down onto a barstool. "I can't believe this," she said again.

"Well, believe it, girl!" Gertie said, laughing. "You and that husband of yours have put Braesburg on the map!"

Gayla pushed to her feet. "I've got to show this to him," she muttered, trying not to let her hopes outweigh her common sense. She scooped the papers up off the floor, then grabbed the one from the counter. "I'll bring your papers back, Gertie. I promise," she called over her shoulder as she headed for the door.

Gayla made the trip home in record time and hit the back door, running. "Brett!" she called. "Brett! Where are you?" Holding the newspapers to her heaving breasts, she paused, listening, and heard the muffled sound of water running through the pipes overhead.

Clutching the newspapers in her hands, she charged for the stairs, taking them two at a time. "Brett!" she called again, and pushed open the bedroom door. "Brett, you won't believe—"

She stopped abruptly just inside the door. Her fingers curled into the newspapers while the smile slowly melted from her face. On the bed sat Brett's duffel bag, its sides bulging, the sleeve of a blue denim shirt hanging haphazardly from its gaping opening. Slowly, she looked around the room. The dresser drawer where he'd kept his personal items hung open, empty but for a satin sachet of lavender she kept there for the guests. Padded hangers swung from the closet rod, stripped of the shirts and jeans she had washed and ironed over the past months.

The bathroom door opened and she jerked her gaze to it, watching, her stomach rising to her throat, as Brett stepped through, bare-chested, rubbing his wet hair with a towel, his shaving kit tucked under his arm. When he saw her, he stopped, too, a guilty frown puckering one corner of his mouth.

"I see you saw the papers," he said, nodding at the newspapers she clutched in her hands.

"Yes," she said, unsure how her lips even formed the simple response.

"Marty called. The same stories are running in the Kansas City papers. The employees at headquarters are running scared for fear they're all going to have to move or lose their jobs. I've got to get up there and calm everybody down."

"How long will you be gone?" she asked, her voice almost a whisper.

He tossed the shaving kit into the duffel bag, then grabbed the ends of the towel in tight fists as he faced her, his expression grim.

"My six months are up, Gayla."

The newspapers slipped from her hands. She closed her eyes against the pain. He was leaving for good. He wouldn't be coming back.

She knelt to gather the newspapers from the floor, struggling for breath, not wanting to make this any worse than it already was. She wanted to rail at him, to scream and hit and throw things. But she couldn't. He'd never pretended that his stay in Braesburg, or their marriage, was anything but temporary.

She rose, neatly folded the papers and laid them on the dresser, then slowly turned back to him. "I guess I won't be needing this anymore," she said and slipped the gold wedding band from her finger. She held it out to him.

Frowning, Brett hesitated for a moment, then plucked the ring from her palm, turning the gold band around and around between his fingers, avoiding her gaze, looking unsure what to do or say.

But Gayla had something to say—something she'd kept inside for months and months. "I love you, Brett," she said softly. His gaze flicked to hers, his eyes filled with a mixture of dread and panic. A wisp of a smile played on her lips at his reaction, although her heart threatened to break. "I didn't tell you before, because I was afraid if I did, you'd leave." She lifted a shoulder in a shrug. "But you're leaving now, anyway, so it doesn't matter."

His eyes darkened with guilt. "Gayla, I'm sorry," he murmured.

Digging deep, she found the strength she needed to survive this last confrontation. She lifted her chin.

"You don't have anything to be sorry for, Brett. You never pretended that our marriage was anything but temporary." Then, before he could see the tears that threatened, she turned and walked from the room.

Gertie took one look at Gayla's face and ushered her to a booth in the back. Snatching napkins from the table dispenser, she closed Gayla's fingers around the wad. "Honey, what's happened?" Gertie asked in concern.

Gayla dabbed at her eyes, then her nose. "Brett's gone," she said, her eyes immediately filling up again.

"Gone?" Gertie repeated, perplexed. "Gone where?"

"Back to Kansas City."

"You mean he left you?" Gertie cried in dismay.

Gayla could only nod.

"Why, that sorry, low-down, no-good—"

Gayla grabbed Gertie's hand. "No, Gertie. It's not what you think."

"When a man ups and leaves his wife, I know what I think! I think he's—"

"I'm not his wife."

That silenced Gertie when little else would...but only for a moment. "Well, of course you're his wife," she said impatiently. "He married you, didn't he?"

"Yes," Gayla replied, then decided that with Brett on his way out of town, the secrecy behind their marriage no longer mattered. "But it was simply a marriage of convenience," she explained. "In his will Ned left me the right of residency at Parker House until my death or until I married. He also stipulated that Parker House couldn't be sold unless the heir maintained residency for six months. In order to meet both requirements of the will, Brett suggested that we marry."

"And you agreed?" Gertie asked in disbelief.

"Yes. You know how much Ned loved Parker House and how he wanted to keep it in his family. I had hoped that if Brett stayed here for a while, somehow he'd grow to love it as much as Ned."

"But I saw the two of you," Gertie cried. "You acted just like newlyweds. Just yesterday I saw the two of you standing out on the street kissing like you were the only two people left in the world."

Gayla blushed and averted her gaze. "We did become physically involved," she admitted, then lifted her gaze, her eyes flooded with tears. "But I loved him, Gertie. I still do."

"Does he love you?"

Gayla pressed the wad of tissues beneath her nose. "I don't know," she muttered miserably, her sobs increasing. "I thought so, though he's never said as much. But it doesn't matter now. He's gone, and he won't be coming back."

Gertie reached over and patted Gayla's hand. "There, there," she soothed. "Crying never solved a problem." She patted again, until Gayla had calmed somewhat. "So what are you going to do? Will you stay on as innkeeper at Parker House?" she asked.

"No," Gayla said with a shake of her head. "Brett is giving the property to the city."

''Where will you go?''

Gayla turned to gaze out the window. ''I don't know,'' she murmured.

Again, Gertie reached over and patted Gayla's hand. ''Why don't you move in with me for a while?'' she suggested. ''Just until you get on your feet. God knows, I've got the room.''

John Thomas didn't waste any time preparing the divorce papers Brett had requested before he'd left town. He figured the sooner Gayla dealt with all the legal issues surrounding her marriage, the sooner she could forget Brett and get on with her life. It broke his heart to see her looking so forlorn and alone.

With the papers tucked inside his coat, he went to Gertie's Diner where he knew Gayla was working. The doorbell jingled as he entered and Gayla glanced up from behind the counter where she was filling saltshakers during the afternoon lull. Their gazes met and a soft smile curved her lips. ''Hi, John.''

He quickly crossed to the counter. ''Hello, Gayla. Got time for a cup of coffee?''

''I'll make the time.'' Setting aside the saltshaker, she filled two cups and motioned John to follow her to a booth under the front window where sunshine warmed the vinyl seats.

Once settled, she lifted her cup to her lips, taking a careful sip while studying John over its rim. ''What brings you over in the middle of the afternoon?'' she asked, setting the cup aside.

John frowned as he drew the papers from his coat pocket. ''I have your divorce papers.''

He laid the papers in the center of the table and Gayla stared at them, unable to bring herself to touch them. She heaved a shuddery breath. ''He certainly didn't waste any time, did he?''

''No reason to drag it out,'' John replied. ''I just need your signature so I can file the papers at the courthouse.'' He unfolded the document and quickly turned to the page where Gayla's signature was required.

Gayla nervously wet her lips as she rubbed her palms up and down her thighs before accepting the pen John offered. *Gayla Matthews Sinclair.* Her hand shaking, she signed the name she had carried for a little over six months, thus severing her last tie to Brett. She handed John his pen, then sank against the back of the seat, feeling suddenly empty.

John quickly refolded the papers and stuffed them back into his jacket pocket, putting them out of sight. ''There is one other matter,'' he said, wanting to take care of everything as quickly as possible. ''Brett deeded Parker House over to you.''

Gayla's eyes widened in shock. ''He what?''

''He deeded Parker House over to you,'' he repeated and added, ''Along with the rest of Ned's estate.''

Gayla could only stare, remembering Brett's adamancy that the entire estate would go to the city when his six months were up. Another memory quickly surfaced and she closed her eyes, seeing again the two, crisp one-hundred-dollar bills Brett had left lying on the pillow the first time he'd left her. The anger that she needed in order to heal, bubbled forth, cauterizing the open wound Brett had left on her heart. Did he think that he could absolve his guilty conscience by giving her Parker House? If so, he had another think coming! Gayla Matthews accepted charity from no one.

"I won't accept it," she said, her voice trembling in anger.

"But, Gayla," John began, trying to get her to listen to reason. "Ned would have wanted you to have it."

"No, Ned wanted Parker House to remain in his family. As much as I loved and cared for him, I am not his family."

"But what am I supposed to tell Brett?"

She rose from the table, her chin tipped higher than John had seen it since Brett had left town.

"You can tell him that I don't want or need his charity," she retorted, then turned and strode away.

Gertie walked in from the kitchen, carrying a load of clean cups and saucers and saw Gayla standing at the front door to the diner, staring across the street. After hefting the load of dishes onto the countertop, she gathered the skirt of her apron into her hands and dried them as she went to stand behind Gayla.

"What are you staring at so hard?" she asked, straining to see what Gayla found so interesting.

Gayla nodded at the small shop across the street where a faded sign on the window proclaimed Goodson's Shoe Repair. "Do you think Mrs. Goodson would lease me the old shoe-repair store?"

Gertie puckered her lips thoughtfully. "I don't know why not. She's certainly not doing anything with it." She smoothed her apron skirt across her round middle. "What did you have in mind for the place?"

Gayla replied absently, "A bakery, I think. Nothing big or fancy, just a simple shop where I could bake for others like I do for you." She cocked her head, studying the location. "I have a little money saved, plus I think I could get a small-business loan from the bank to help me get started."

Gertie didn't know what had transpired between Gayla and John, but whatever it was, she was thrilled—even if by opening a bakery right across the street from her diner, Gayla managed to steal a little of her business.

Gertie caught the strings of Gayla's apron and gave them a tug. "You're dang right the bank will make you a loan," she said, peeling the apron from around Gayla's waist. "And if they won't, I sure as heck will." She gave Gayla a little shove in what she prayed was the right direction. "Now, you get on over to Mrs. Goodson's house and ask her about leasing that shop."

Brett lay sprawled on the couch in the den of his mother's Kansas City home, his arm slung across his closed eyes. The house was his now, part of his inheritance from Christine Sinclair, but he still thought of it as his mother's. It was the house he'd grown up in, although he had no particular affection for the place.

His chest rose and fell in a weary sigh. He was lonely. Lonelier than he'd ever been in his entire life, and that was saying a lot, because he'd spent most of his early years alone, without the camaraderie of siblings, and isolated from his parents by their constant bickering. The walls reverberated with the unhappiness that had filled the house. When he was young, Brett had sought the sanctuary of his room and the companionship of an old junkyard dog he'd adopted, named Fred. But Fred was gone now, which left Brett with no one but himself for company.

And at the moment he would have preferred anyone's company to his own.

He rolled into a sitting position, propping his elbows on his knees and his forehead against the heels of his hands. God, how he missed Gayla. The sound of her humming in the kitchen while she baked. The scent of roses that seemed to trail behind her wherever she went. The music of her laughter, the thrill of her touch. Sleeping beside her, waking up with her. Unconsciously, he pressed a hand over his heart and rubbed. Would the pain never stop? he wondered. Would the need to see her, touch her, hold her never leave him?

He closed his eyes against the memory of her standing at the door to the room they'd shared, her face drained of color, her eyes wide in horror when she'd found him packing. Tears had brimmed in her eyes and her hand had shook as she'd lifted it to brush away the tears, refusing to let him see her cry. He hadn't wanted to hurt her. From the beginning, he'd tried to remain distant, and when that had failed, he'd purposely never made any promises he knew he couldn't keep.

But he hadn't been able to stop himself from falling in love with her, as hard as he'd fought that probability.

He scooped the empty beer can from the coffee table. His face distorted with anger, his body shaking in silent rage, he squeezed the can, crumpling it within his hand. Rearing back, he threw the flattened disk as hard as he could, sending it flying across the room to crack against the far wall.

"Damn you, Gayla!" he roared, his hands fisted at the heavens. "Why did you make me love you?" The strength seeped from him and he fell back against the sofa, burying his face in his hands. "Oh, God, why did you make me love you?"

Brett's secretary stuck her head in his door. "You have a visitor."

Brett didn't even glance up. "Get rid of 'em."

"It's that lawyer from Braesburg."

His head came up at that, his hands stilled on the papers he held. "John Thomas?" he asked. He hadn't heard from John since he'd left Braesburg more than a month before.

"Yes, I believe that was the name he gave."

Brett waved her toward the door. "Send him in."

He stood while Maxine ushered John into the office,

then stretched his hand across the desk, a smile broadening on his face. "John," he said in greeting. "What are you doing in Kansas City?"

John shook Brett's hand, then lifted his briefcase to the top of Brett's desk. "I thought perhaps this would be better taken care of in person."

He flipped opened his briefcase and lifted out several folders. From the first he drew a thick legal document. "Here's your copy of the divorce papers," he said and dropped it on the desk in front of Brett. "Gayla didn't contest it, and I've filed it with the court." He replaced the folder and opened a second. "And these," he said with a sigh, as he drew out several documents, "are the deeds to Parker House, the hardware store and all the other assets that made up Ned's estate."

Frowning, Brett looked from the papers to John. "But I told you to transfer all this to Gayla's name."

"I did," John replied, one corner of his mouth puckering in a scowl. "But she wouldn't accept it."

"And why not?" Brett demanded angrily.

John tossed the empty folders back into his briefcase and closed the lid with a snap. He lifted his head, leveling his gaze on Brett's. "She told me to tell you, and I quote, 'I don't need or want his charity.'"

"This isn't charity," Brett argued, waving at the documents littering his desk. "Hell, she earned this and more."

John dragged his briefcase from the top of the desk. "Maybe that's part of the problem," he said, his voice resigned. "Maybe Gayla did what she did for a reason other than personal gain."

After John left, Brett sat down in his chair and stared at the papers before him. As hard as he tried, he couldn't get John's parting comment out of his mind. He hadn't left Gayla Ned's estate as some act of charity! Dammit, she had worked for years for nothing but room and board, taking care of his grandfather and that huge old house the old man had refused to give up. She deserved whatever wealth his grandfather had left behind.

She loved Parker House—he knew she did. So why did she refuse to accept the property? Did she hate him that much?

He pressed a hand over his heart at the thought. She didn't hate him, he told himself. She couldn't. She loved him. She'd told him so herself. His fingers curled into a fist against his heart. A gift, he slowly realized. She'd offered him the gift of her love and, like a fool, he'd turned it down.

But maybe it wasn't too late, he told himself. Maybe it wasn't too late to claim her love.

But first he had a few things he had to take care of. Things he should have taken care of long before now.

He punched the intercom that connected his office with that of his secretary. "Maxine," he said. "Call a board meeting for four o'clock this afternoon, then come to my office and bring a pad and pen with you. We've got some work to do."

Two days. That was all the time it took for Brett to present his resignation to Sinclair's board, list his mother's house for sale, arrange for the things he wanted to keep to be placed in storage, and head for Braesburg. But even at that, the two days seemed like an eternity. Brett was anxious to go home.

When he arrived at Parker House, he stopped his truck on the circular drive in front and turned off the ignition. Angling his body sideways on the seat, he peered through the passenger window at the two-story stone house. The windows gleamed, reflecting back at him the sunlight that shone overhead. The white wicker rockers scattered about the porch slowly swayed in the gentle afternoon breeze, as if nodding a greeting to Brett.

Seven months ago he'd parked in this same spot and looked at Parker House for the first time, his sole purpose in doing so to see the house where his mother grew up before he gave it away to the city. At that time, his mind had been filled with lies and his heart with hate.

Today, he had other things on his mind. And his heart—Well, he'd left it somewhere inside this old house. And today, he had returned to claim it. Never mind that his hands shook, or that his legs felt as if someone had bored a hole in his big toe and drained the strength right out of him. He was home. And damn, but it felt good!

Shouldering open the door of the truck, he strode toward the front door, anxious to see Gayla, to hold her, to tell her what a fool he'd been for leaving and how much he loved her.

He rang the bell, shifting nervously from one foot to the other. After a moment, he punched the button again, then squinted to peer through the door's etched glass, but he didn't see or hear any sign of Gayla inside. Disappointed, he stuffed his hands in his pockets and turned back to his truck. She couldn't be far, he told himself. He would just mosey over to Gertie's and have himself a cup of coffee, then he would give her a call.

The bell over the entrance to the diner jingled as Brett pushed through the door. He paused, looking around on the odd chance that Gayla might be one of the customers. Not seeing her, he strode for the counter and slid onto a stool. Gertie shuffled past, her hands filled with a tray of dirty dishes.

"Hi, Gertie," he said. "How about a cup of coffee?"

She grunted something unintelligible and kept right on going, pushing a hip against the swinging door that led to the kitchen, and disappearing on the other side. Puzzled, Brett frowned, then looked around the diner. Several pairs of eyes were focused on him, but when he turned, the people all dropped their gazes or quickly looked the other way—but not before he felt the sting of their animosity. *What in the hell's wrong with everybody?* he wondered, puzzled by their odd behavior.

He caught a glimpse of Ted Baxter sitting farther down the counter. Leaning forward, he hollered, "Hey, Ted! How's it going?"

Ted didn't even look up, but kept right on eating.

Feeling as if he'd just stepped into "The Twilight Zone," Brett slid off the stool and headed for the door.

Outside he paused, wondering what had come over the townspeople, and noticed a crowd of people gathered across the street. As he watched, a reporter from the local paper directed the crowd to move back so that he could take a picture. Aligned almost directly behind the reporter, once the people moved, Brett had a direct view of the activities. A long, wide strip of ribbon stretched across the storefront...and behind it stood Gayla, with a pair of scissors poised over the wide ribbon, smiling into the camera.

The sun gleamed on her blond hair, creating a halo effect around her, making her look even more like an angel than he remembered. Above her head, a banner waved in the gentle breeze. Grand Opening Sweet Memories. He strained for a look into the shop window behind her and saw pedestals bearing pies, cakes, and an assortment of breads.

A retail store? Gayla had opened a retail store?

The scissors sliced through the ribbon, the camera flashed and the crowd broke out with cheers and applause. Laughing, Gayla glanced up, her face radiant...until her gaze met Brett's across the width of the street. At the sight of him she stiffened visibly, the smile melting from her face. He lifted his hand to wave to her, but before his hand reached hip level, she turned away.

Brett felt as if a hot knife had stabbed through his chest. He forced himself to take a deep breath. She was angry with him, he told himself. And rightfully so. Once he explained why he had left so abruptly and told her of his feelings for her, everything would be okay.

He frowned at the crowd that surrounded her. Later, he decided. He wouldn't try to talk to her with half of Braesburg standing by and listening.

He made a circuit of the downtown area, noting all the changes that had been made in the month he'd been away. By the time he wound his way back to Sweet Memories, the crowd was gone. Brett stepped across the threshold of the shop, pausing for a moment to let his eyes grow accustomed to the change in light. Her shop smelled like the kitchen at Parker House, with odors of yeast, vanilla and cinnamon tangling for dominance in the air. Below it all hung the scent of roses. Brett inhaled deeply, letting memories wash over him—all of them sweet.

"May I help you?"

The sound of Gayla's voice drew him back to the present. She stood behind the counter, her hands buried deep in the pockets of a crisp white linen apron.

"I hope so," he replied, and moved to the counter, wanting to grab her and hug her and tell her how much he'd missed her. But he knew she probably wasn't ready to hear that just yet. Instead he offered her a half smile, hoping to tease a smile out of her in return. "I was looking for a place to stay the night."

Her eyes remained fixed on his for a moment, before she tore her gaze away. She drew her hands from her pockets to dust crumbs from the glass case filled with desserts. "Sweet Memories is a bakery, not a hotel."

Her answer wasn't the one he'd wanted to hear. "I was hoping I could stay at Parker House with you," he said softly, trying to keep his voice low so as not to attract the attention of the other customers.

He thought he detected the slightest wavering—a quiver in her lower lip, a softening in her eyes. But she seemed to catch herself and her chin came up, her spine stiffened.

"You'll have to see John Thomas if you want to stay at Parker House," she said briskly and flicked the crumbs into a wastebasket. "Was there anything else I can do for you?"

The tight smile she offered him fell about a mile short of touching her eyes.

"Gayla, please," Brett murmured, stretching a hand across the counter in silent entreaty. "Can't we talk?"

She stepped back to avoid his touch, holding her arms just out of reach.

"I have nothing to say to you. Now, if you'll excuse me," she said, her voice tight with barely controlled anger, "I have cookies in the oven that need to come out."

Before Brett could stop her, she disappeared behind a curtained doorway. "Gayla!" he called after her. "Gayla, please, I need to talk to you!" He heard a snicker from behind him and wheeled to find several customers watching him in undisguised amusement. Angered to discover an audience had witnessed his rejection, he strode around the counter, headed for the curtained doorway Gayla had disappeared behind.

I was hoping I could stay with you at Parker House.

Fuming, Gayla jerked a tray of cookies from the oven, then slammed the oven door. Of all the unmitigated gall! Did he think he could just waltz into town and expect her to crawl right back in bed with him? Well, if he did, he certainly had another think coming! She'd made a fool of herself over him once. She wouldn't make that mistake again.

She shoved the tray onto the counter and angrily stripped off her oven mitts. And what was he doing in Braesburg anyway? she wondered irritably as she snatched up a spatula and shoveled cookies from the tray. Surely all the business associated with closing Ned's estate could be dealt with by phone or by mail.

She gave herself a hard shake, angry with herself for giving his reappearance in town that much thought. She didn't have time to worry about Brett Sinclair, she told herself firmly. She had a business to manage.

"Gayla?"

She jerked her head up at the unexpected sound of his voice, the cookie she'd just levered from the sheet sliding from the spatula to the floor. Her lips tightened defensively. "What do you want?"

"To talk to you."

She brushed past him. "I've already told you, I have nothing to say."

He caught her arm, stopping her. "Well, I do."

She turned, her gaze fixed on the hold he had on

her arm. He released her with a sigh. There was so much to say, he wasn't sure where to begin. "I didn't deed Parker House to you as an act of charity. You more than earned it through all the years you took care of Ned."

Gayla hadn't thought he could hurt her anymore. She was wrong. "I took care of Ned because I loved him, and for no other reason."

"I know that." Brett let out another sigh, sure that he was making things worse between them instead of better, but unsure how to make things right. "I was wrong about a lot of things, Gayla. I should never have left Braesburg." He shook his head. "But I guess I had to leave in order to realize what I had found here with you."

"And what was that?" she asked, trying to remain detached, but with her heart threatening to split apart in her chest at any moment.

"Happiness. Peace."

She felt herself weakening. All the things she had hoped he would find. She dug her nails into her palms, fighting for the strength to keep from knuckling under, to keep from throwing herself into his arms. He had hurt her once. She wasn't sure she could survive if he hurt her again.

"I'm glad you found those things, Brett," she said honestly. "Everyone deserves to be happy. Now, if you'll excuse me," she finished, tears burning her eyes, knowing that she couldn't listen to any more. "I have customers waiting." She picked up the tray of cookies and ducked through the curtained doorway.

Ten

The news of Brett's return to Braesburg swept through the town, drawing more furor than the return of the prodigal son. They'd all heard the truth behind Brett and Gayla's marriage, about her agreeing to marry him just so he could meet all the stipulations of the will and settle Ned's estate. Those who remembered Christine Parker said that Brett had inherited his mother's selfishness. Others said that Gayla was a fool for going along with his scheme. But they all agreed on one thing: Brett Sinclair had used one of their own for his personal gain.

Once again, Gayla found herself the topic of town gossip, but this time there was a difference. She was the heroine of their tales...and Brett Sinclair was the indisputable villain.

Determined to prove to Gayla that he was in Braesburg to stay, Brett settled into Parker House quickly, and did what Gayla hadn't been able to bring herself to do in the seven months since Ned's death: he went through Ned's belongings, separating those things he deemed important and boxing the rest for donation.

The task was a difficult one, with years of accumulation to go through, but Brett had the time. Without the burden of Sinclair's weighing on him, and with Gayla refusing to see him or talk to him, he had little else to do. He would bide his time, he told himself, allowing her the opportunity to see that he was in Braesburg to stay. Convincing Gayla that she could trust him would take time, but, hey, at the moment, he had time to spare.

And he had a plan.

Gayla was certain that within the month they would have to commit her. She couldn't take much more. Brett seemed determined to drive her crazy.

She shoved the tray of cinnamon rolls onto a rack in the display case, refusing to glance Brett's way.

He sat with his back to her shop window, as he had every morning for the past week, watching her every move while he drank a cup of coffee and nibbled his way through a cinnamon roll, driving her slowly crazy.

He never said anything more intimate than "Good morning, Gayla" when he arrived or "Have a nice day, Gayla" when he left, yet she felt stripped naked the entire time he sat in her shop.

But maybe because that was what she wanted to be. Naked. Alone with Brett.

She slid the glass door on the display case closed with such force the plates inside rattled, then moved through the curtained doorway to the kitchen beyond. Once out of his sight, she pressed her fevered forehead against the cold metal of the refrigerator door. *God, please,* she prayed silently, *I can't take much more.*

Gayla heard the bell over the entrance jingle and lifted her head, listening, hoping to hear the scrape of Brett's boots leaving her shop. But the lilt of feminine voices told her someone was coming, not going.

"Good morning, Mrs. Mason, Mrs. Collier," she heard Brett say. "And what are you two beautiful ladies doing out so early this morning?"

It was all Gayla could do to keep from gagging at the syrupy sweetness in his tone. It pleased her enormously to know that he couldn't have found two women less willing to listen to his line of bull than Clara Mason and Sarah Collier. They'd been known to take a man down with the sharpness of their tongues for a lesser cause. She waited for one of them to put him in his place.

"Why, Brett," Clara simpered. "If you haven't just made my day!" The sound of their girlish tittering made Gayla's temperature rise another degree.

Unable to stand it any longer, she bulldozed her way through the curtain. Glaring at Brett, she heaved a deep breath before she turned to greet her customers. "Good morning, Mrs. Mason, Mrs. Collier," she said pleasantly. "What can I do for you today?"

''Good morning, Gayla,'' Mrs. Mason replied, turning her attention to the glass display case. ''Clara and I are hostessing the bridge group this morning, and we were thinking about serving something sweet along with the coffee.'' She pointed a finger at a sour-cream coffee cake. ''How much is that?'' she asked.

''Eight ninety-five.''

''That'll do,'' Mrs. Mason said primly. ''Could you box it up, please?''

''I'll be happy to.'' Gayla pulled the cake from the rack and levered it into a box with the Sweet Memories logo stamped across its top. From the corner of her eye she watched Brett rise to his feet. He picked up the small tray holding his empty coffee cup and plate and carried it to the counter.

''That was a mighty good cinnamon roll, Gayla,'' he said appreciatively. Plucking his hat from the brass-pegged tree by the door, he pulled it on, then hooked a finger on its brim. ''You ladies have a nice day,'' he said in parting.

Clara Mason and Sarah Collier watched him leave, all but drooling. When the door closed behind him, the ladies released a collective sigh. ''My, such manners and handsome to boot,'' Clara Mason said.

''Inside and out,'' Sarah Collier added. ''Did you know that he donated all of Ned's personal effects to the Community Closet over at the church?'' At Clara's look of surprise, she nodded her head. ''He certainly did. And can you imagine a young man like him taking on such a task?'' She made a tsking sound with her tongue. ''Cleaning out closets and drawers. Most men would consider that a woman's work.'' She shifted her gaze to Gayla, and Gayla quickly busied herself folding down the sides of the cake box and applying tape, pretending that she wasn't interested in their conversation.

''Mark my word,'' Sarah said with a knowing look at Clara. ''He'll make some woman a fine husband one day.''

Clara Mason and Sarah Collier's visit to Sweet Memories was only the beginning. Gayla lost count over the next week of the number of people who dropped by her shop to extol Brett Sinclair's virtues. Did she know that he'd offered to buy the church a new pipe organ? one do-gooder asked. Or had she heard that he'd mowed the widow Baker's lawn the day before?

The crowning blow had come on Friday afternoon when Ted Baxter had stopped by to show her a copy of the *Wall Street Journal* and an article that announced the resignation of Brett Sinclair as president of Sinclair Corporation.

By closing time, Gayla was fit to be tied. What was he up to? she stewed.

After locking the shop she headed for Gertie's Diner, wanting to be with someone who shared her distrust of the man. She knew she could depend on Gertie for the support she needed.

Scooping the coffeepot from the hot plate behind the counter, she poured herself a cup and wished she were a drinking woman. She would like nothing better than to toss back a glass of whiskey right now. Maybe that would make Brett's sudden change of character a little easier to swallow.

"Gertie!" she called. "Where are you?"

"Back here," came Gertie's muffled reply.

Sipping at her coffee, Gayla rounded the counter and pushed through the swinging door. She jerked to a stop, hot coffee sloshing over her hand—but she didn't even feel its sting. She was numbed by the sight of Brett sitting opposite Gertie at the scarred kitchen table, playing cards fanned in his hands, an unlit cigar clamped between his teeth.

Without acknowledging Gayla's entrance, Brett leaned forward and tossed a handful of change onto the pile of coins in the center of the table. "I'll see your quarter and raise you fifty cents," he said, then leaned back and watched Gertie over his cards, his face a closed mask.

Gertie's lips puckered and she narrowed an eye at him. With a sigh, she laid down her cards. "I fold," she announced, showing a pair of queens.

Chuckling, Brett scraped the money from the table. Gertie snagged his wrist. "Just out of curiosity, what did you have?"

Brett turned his cards over, revealing a measly pair of threes. Gertie threw up her hands, blustering, "Well, I'll be a son of a gun. If you didn't inherit your granddaddy's poker face, I'll eat my hat."

Laughing, Brett gathered up the cards. "Want to play another hand?"

"Shoot, no!" Gertie exclaimed. "You've already

stripped me of a week's worth of tips.'' She pressed her arthritic knuckles to the table and pushed to her feet. One look at Gayla's stricken face and she pursed her lips guiltily as she headed for the swinging door and the diner beyond. ''Pooh, it was only an innocent little card game,'' she muttered as she pushed through the door.

Brett split the cards and riffled them between his thumbs, the sound drawing Gayla's gaze to his hands. He turned the cards on end and repeated the process. ''Interested in a game?'' he asked without looking up.

The deft movements of his hands on the cards did something to Gayla's insides, inciting memories of the feel of those same hands on her skin. ''No,'' she murmured, unable to tear her gaze away. ''I just stopped by to tell Gertie I was going home.''

Fanning the cards between his fingers like the pleats of an accordion, Brett glanced up. He saw the heat in her eyes, and knew that despite all her posturing otherwise, she wanted him as badly as he wanted her. Right then and there, he decided to hell with patience. One way or another, he was going to make her listen to him and convince her of his love.

Shuffling the cards to one hand, he thumped them against the table, then laid them aside and rose. ''I'll drive you home.''

Her gaze leaped to his.

''No!'' Gayla blurted out, then forced herself to repeat more calmly, ''No, really, there's no need. Gertie's house isn't far.''

But he was already at her side, cupping her elbow

in his hand. He guided her through the swinging door to the dining room. "I'm going to see Gayla home," Brett said as they passed by Gertie.

"Better watch him," Gertie said to Gayla, trying not to smile. "He might have a card or two up his sleeve."

Brett held the door open, waiting while Gayla passed in front of him. Over Gayla's head, he shot Gertie a wink, his grin broadening when she gave him a thumbs-up sign.

Once outside, Gayla paused while she waited for Brett to unlock his truck. Night closed around them, adding an intimacy to their nearness that Gayla didn't need or want. She was already more aware of Brett Sinclair than was healthy. Frustrated by her inability to control her body's craving for him, she climbed into the truck, then plastered herself against the door, putting as much distance as possible between her and Brett.

The air in the cab of the truck crackled with sexual energy as he backed out of the parking space and headed down Main Street. Gayla wondered if Brett was as aware of that fact as she. Heat from his body pulsed against her, making breathing difficult.

With her nose pressed to the passenger window and her eyes closed against temptation, Gayla wasn't aware of the direction they'd taken until Brett stopped the truck and she opened her eyes. Parker House loomed before her.

"Brett," she warned in a low voice.

"I just need to get something," he said and hopped from the truck.

Gayla stared at Parker House, emotion making her throat raw. The house held so many memories for her. Some good, some bad, but the ones that came quickest to mind, the ones most dear, all centered around Brett. Her eyes misting, she nearly fell out of the truck when Brett opened her door.

"What are you—" But before she could demand an explanation for his actions, he had tugged her from the truck and slung her over his shoulder, fireman-style.

"Brett!" she screamed. "You put me down right this instant!"

"I will, Gayla," he replied. "Just as soon as we get inside."

But once inside, he didn't stop. He marched right up the stairs with Gayla's head dangling at his hip, her fists pounding against his rear end.

In Ned's bedroom, the room he now claimed as his own, Brett dropped her onto the bed. She came up spitting and scratching, madder than a wet cat. "How dare you!" she screeched and levered herself to a sitting position, shoving against his chest. Brett shoved right back.

She fell back, flattening her palms against the mattress to catch herself. Her mouth dropped open as she stared up at him, shocked by his he-man tactics.

Brett folded his arms across his chest. "Sorry for the abduction scene, but it seemed like the only way

I would ever be able to get you alone long enough for you to listen to me.''

Her chin closed with a snap of teeth. She lifted her foot and planted it against his chest, shoving with all her weight. Brett didn't budge an inch. He simply caught her at the ankle and moved her foot aside, stepping into the vee he'd created between her legs.

''I thought we could do this civilly,'' he said. ''But I can see that you aren't ready to be reasonable.''

Gayla didn't like the look in his eye. Digging her heels into the mattress, she started backing away. Brett dove to catch her before she could make good her escape, pinning her beneath his weight. She opened her mouth to scream, but he quickly closed his mouth over hers, absorbing her cry of indignant rage. Gayla fisted her hands against his chest, struggling to free herself. With his lips still on hers, he caught her hands in his and dragged them above her head. Once he held her immobile, he softened his mouth on hers.

Gayla could have withstood his anger, could have resisted whatever brute force he used to try to bend her to his will and would have fought back with every ounce of her strength. But she couldn't fight the tenderness of his lips on hers, the familiar taste, the heat that never failed to fire a similar response deep within her.

Her own lips parted beneath his in a moan of surrender.

Slowly, Brett drew away. She opened her eyes to meet his gaze, her chest heaving.

"Why are you doing this?" she asked, her voice thick with tears.

"Because I love you."

He felt the tension move through her as she fought to deny his words. "It's true, Gayla," he said, tightening his hands on her wrists. "I do love you, you have to believe that."

She wanted to believe him. Oh, God, how she wanted to believe. But she'd offered him her heart once and he'd walked away. She squeezed her eyes shut tight as if she could block out the sound of his voice, the emotion that was threatening to suck the life from her. "Please, don't do this, Brett. Please," she nearly sobbed. "I don't want to hurt anymore."

"Oh, Gayla, honey," he soothed. "I don't want to hurt you. I never wanted to hurt you."

"But you did," she said, unable to stop the tears that streamed down her face. "When you left for Kansas City, you broke my heart."

"I swear I thought I was doing what was best for you," he said.

"Best for me?" she cried. "How could you possibly think that your leaving was best for me?"

"Because I wasn't sure I had what it took to make you happy."

Her breath hitched once, twice, while she stared at him, unable to believe that he could think such a thing. "But I was happy, Brett. Didn't you see that?"

"Yes...no." Frustrated, he pushed himself off her to pace away from the bed. Digging his fingers through his hair, he whirled back. "I knew *I* was happy, and that's what scared me. I had grown to depend on you, to need you. And I've never let anyone get that close or mean that much before. I thought I knew what loneliness was before, but I didn't. Not until I had to live without you.''

''Oh, Brett,'' she said, her heart breaking all over again. She pushed to sit on the edge of the bed, pressing her fingertips against her temples.

He dropped down beside her. He took her hand and felt a small victory when she didn't jerk away. ''Gayla,'' he said, lifting his gaze to hers, ''I love you. Please believe me. And this time, I swear, I'm here to stay.''

Her throat raw, she searched his gaze, wanting to believe him, but scared to death to expose her heart again. ''What's changed, Brett?'' she finally asked.

''Me.'' His shoulders rose and fell on a sigh. ''I realized that I've spent my entire life either trying to please my mother or trying to prove something to my father—even after they were gone.'' He shook his head, still unable to believe how blind he'd been. ''I've always considered them both selfish. What I didn't realize was that I was, too.''

He dipped his chin to his chest, his gaze fixed on their joined hands. ''Everything I did, I did because I wanted something from them. Their love, their respect. But nothing ever seemed to be enough. They always withheld their affection and approval and continued to use me as a pawn in their emotional game of chess.'' He cocked his head to look at Gayla. ''You are the only person in my entire life who ever offered me love and expected nothing in return." He smiled ruefully and shook his head again. "Unfortunately, I didn't realize that until John told me you'd refused to accept Parker House or any of Ned's estate. It was then that I realized how truly unselfish you are, that the love you offered me was a gift, mine for the taking."

He inhaled deeply. "I was a fool for leaving, Gayla. I know that now."

She could see how much the admission cost him and the pain he'd suffered in coming to that realization. Her heart opened to him.

He flattened her hand between both of his, almost prayerfully. "I still don't know beans about what it takes to make a home or a family, but if you're willing to give me another chance, and if you can be patient with me while I learn, I swear I'll try my damnedest to make you happy while I'm figuring it all out."

Gayla couldn't imagine hearing a more romantic proposal. She lifted a hand to his cheek, smiling through her tears. "A woman couldn't ask for more."

He drew one knee onto the bed, angling himself until he faced her. He closed his fingers around hers. "I want you to marry me, Gayla."

She couldn't help but laugh. "I think I already did that once."

A grin chipped at one corner of his mouth. "Yeah, but this time we'll do it right."

"And how is that?"

"A real wedding, a honeymoon, the works."

"Oh, Brett," she said, laughing. "I don't need all that."

"You don't?"

"No," she replied softly. She curled her arms around his neck, her voice dipping to a seductive whisper. "All I ever needed or wanted was you."

Her words were exactly what he wanted to hear, but when she would have melted against him, he caught her hands and held her at arm's length. A frown furrowed his brow. "There is just one more thing," he began hesitantly.

Gayla knew real fear. "What?"

"Parker House."

Puzzled, she asked, "What about it?"

"If it's all right with you, I'd rather we didn't operate it as a bed-and-breakfast anymore."

She tried not to smile. "Oh? And may I ask why not?"

He started to respond then saw the teasing gleam that sparkled in her brown eyes. He twisted around, pushing her flat on the bed, and straddled her. "Because when I want to make love to my wife," he said in a low voice as he dipped his head to nip at her neck, "I don't want to have to worry about disturbing the guests."

Laughing, Gayla curled her hands around his neck and pulled his face to hers. "As if you ever did."

The heat was instantaneous, melting away the laughter. "Oh, Gayla," he murmured against her lips. "Together we'll make this old house a home."

* * * * *

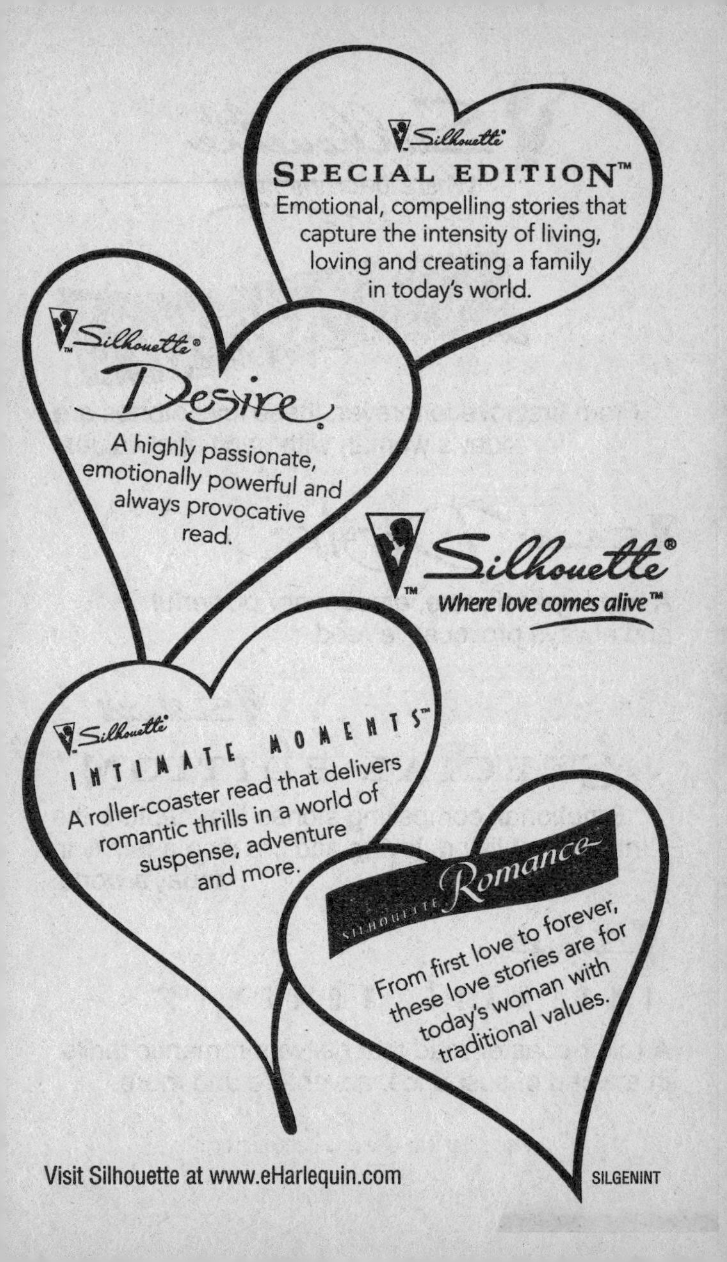
Silhouette
SPECIAL EDITION™
Emotional, compelling stories that capture the intensity of living, loving and creating a family in today's world.
Silhouette®
Desire
A highly passionate, emotionally powerful and always provocative read.
Silhouette®
Where love comes alive™
Silhouette
INTIMATE MOMENTS™
A roller-coaster read that delivers romantic thrills in a world of suspense, adventure and more.
SILHOUETTE Romance
From first love to forever, these love stories are for today's woman with traditional values.
Visit Silhouette at www.eHarlequin.com
SILGENINT